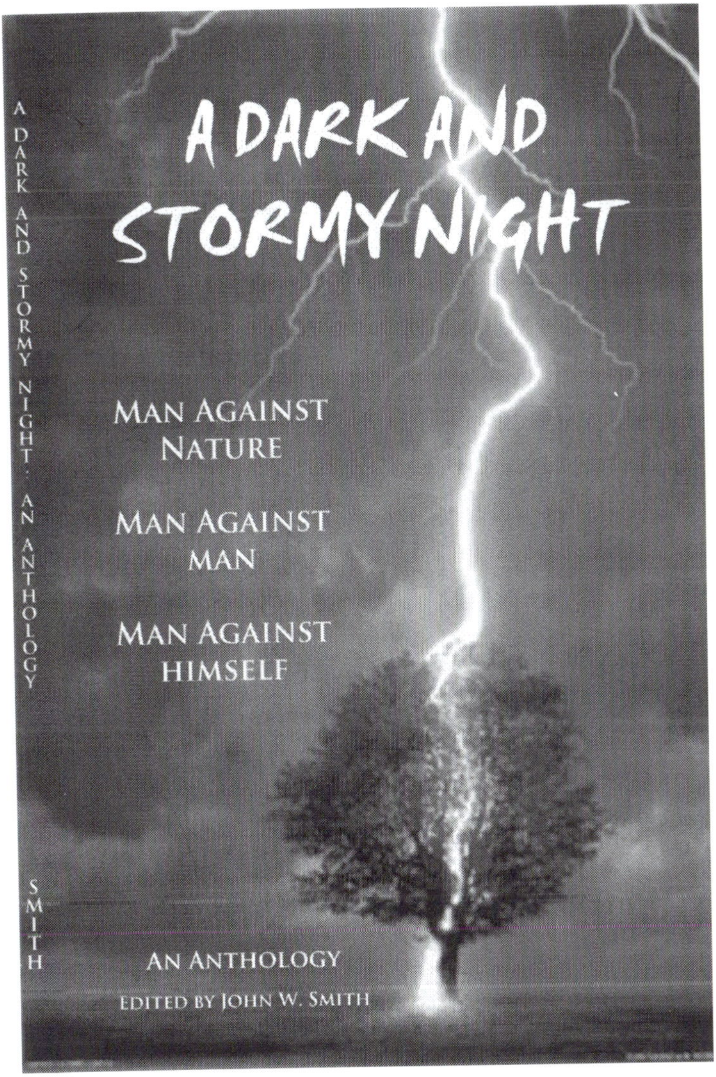
A DARK AND STORMY NIGHT
MAN AGAINST NATURE
MAN AGAINST MAN
MAN AGAINST HIMSELF
AN ANTHOLOGY
EDITED BY JOHN W. SMITH
A DARK AND STORMY NIGHT: AN ANTHOLOGY
SMITH

A Dark and Stormy Night

This book is manufactured in the United States.

This is a work of fiction and a compilation of short stories contributed by several writers. Names, characters, places, and incidents are the product of each author's imagination or are used fictitiously. Any resemblance to actual persons, living or dead is entirely coincidental.

Copyright © 2014 Well Read Press

All rights reserved. No parts of this book may be reproduced in any form or by any electronic or mechanical means including photocopying, recording, or by information retrieval and retrieval systems, without permission in writing from the publisher, except by a reviewer, who may quote brief passages in a review.

All rights reserved.
Published in the United States by Well Read Press

ISBN 978- 0-9891810-2-0
Soft Cover
ISBN 978-0-9891810-3-7
Electronic Edition

FIRST EDITION

Publisher:

Well Read Press
PO Box 12545 State Route 143 Suite C #218
Highland, IL 62249

John Smith
A Dark and Stormy Night: An Anthology

First paperback edition

Advance Praise

When I think of the phrase, "It was a dark and stormy night." The image of Snoopy, Charlie Brown's beagle, comes to mind sitting atop his red doghouse suffering through writer's block.

The storms of life are so dramatic that we feel compelled to write them down, but where do you go from there and how do you make it interesting in 1600 words or less? These writers achieved this task with a variety of interpretations on exactly what comprises a storm to them.

—JoAnn Jenner Bockenfeld. Contributing author of WORDS: An Anthology of Writings

This anthology is something different, a collection with an overriding theme—conflict. It's a subject that offers endless possibilities and true to the premise, the authors take advantage of it. Every kind of conflict imaginable lies between the covers of this book. External conflict, internal conflict, conflict with machines and supernatural beings—it's all here.

Many of the stories are set in supernatural backgrounds or in the suburbs of the supernatural. There are haunted graveyards, uncovered bodies and a creature whose skin resembles the bark of a tree. But, the characters in these stories not only pit themselves against the supernatural but also against machines and each other.

There is some strong narrative writing in these works and some of the authors display a good ear for dialogue. One of the stories has echoes of a Mark Twain adventure story. The writing of some of the authors suggests that they are young writers. There is freshness and an enthusiasm about their work. It will be interesting to see what they do in the years to come.

If you enjoy stories about struggle, whether it is with external demons or internal ones, this book may be for you.

—Mike Warden, author of *Patagonia,* **The Balloon Fair & a Ticket to Far Enough, from** *Words: An Anthology of Short Writings,* **published in 2011,** *The Angel on the Back Stairs, Lake Magazine,* **published in 2012**

It is a dark and stormy night. Outside the wind howls, like a banshee summoning the demons of Hell. Your windows rattle. The rain pelts them unrelentingly. Thunder booms and lightning flashes, the electricity goes out, forcing you to light a candle and sit there ... alone ... as the flickering candle casts weird, shifting shadows on the walls.

You decide to calm your nerves by reading a nice, soothing story... you pick up this book. Wait! Stop! This is not the book you want!

Inside this book, there is no peace, no calm. Inside here are far darker and stormier Nights ... black nights of the soul ... twisted tales of the imagination.

Are you still going to read this book?

If you do, it's your decision. Don't blame me.
I tried to warn you...

—Stan Barker

One word immediately jumped to mind when I reviewed the "Dark and Stormy Night" anthology—suspense. I expected that from a group of stories based on the subject, but three authors come to mind as I think back on the stories. They did a masterful job of grabbing and keeping my attention. They each set the stage with the first sentence and did not let the reader go until the last word of their story.

Ed De Rousse sets the mood by placing the reader in a situation to which everyone can relate ... waking up in the middle of the night and not knowing if you are awake or still asleep. He reinforces the feeling of unease by referring to a horror film everyone will recognize. He prolongs the reader's agony by taking them through a series of actions that only heighten the feeling of anticipated disaster. In the end, he resolves the situation with a truly unexpected twist ... but you should read that yourself.

Sandra Kohler Kohlbrecher takes us on a more fantasy style direction complete with knights, monsters and the indispensable peasants. Suspense is again present early in the story, taking a peaceful setting and destroying it with an unknown terror. She asks questions about the trouble, setting up confusing and different possibilities for the direction of the story. She concludes the situation in the last few words of her story in a truly satisfactory manner.

Mark Laramore takes us on a tour of a space ship through the eyes of a sole survivor of some unknown calamity. He bounces the reader back and forth between what feels like the present and what could be an echo of the past, never letting on which is reality or the workings of a deluded mind. He finally clarifies everything in a unique and unforeseen way.

—George Burbank, co-author of *Colonial Scum*

DEDICATION

This work is dedicated to the writers of this anthology. They were willing to look beyond the title's cliché. They faced the wind, rain and the laughter of others to produce an anthology describing a variety of dark and stormy adventures in life.

This anthology is also dedicated to all writers willing to search new frontiers, extend boundaries and strive to put words on paper that others ask, "Why would you write something like this?"

Carry On and Keep Writing.

ACKNOWLEDGEMENT

I would like to thank BlackWyrm Publishing for planting the idea that created this anthology.

I want to thank my mom for her patience as I planted myself in front of my computer to compile, read, edit, coordinate and select the writers found in this book.

Once again, my thanks to Peggy De Kay and her staff at Darby press for taking the manuscript and turning it into the book you see today.

Thank you, the readers for purchasing this book. I hope you enjoy the stories and that they will inspire you to begin a writing journey into your own *Dark and Stormy Night*.

EDITOR'S NOTE

The phrase, "It was a dark and stormy night," has been mocked and parodied since 1830 when Edward Bulwer-Lytton used it in the opening sentence of his novel, *Paul Clifford*.

The phrase has survived the test of time and has become a popular annual writing contest asking writers to create the worst opening sentence to a novel. It has appeared in movies, comic strips, and many other venues.

While attending the International Writers Summit in Louisville, KY, I purchased an interesting little anthology entitled *Man Made Troubles*. This work contained nine short stories featuring the Frankenstein monster. The stories were limited to a maximum of 1,500 words. I bought the book and read it three times. My mind began to wander … a themed anthology would be a fun project to do. I began to consider all types of themes that could be used to produce an easy to read, enjoyable anthology. Weeks passed and nothing came to mind. Then several months later at a regular meeting of one of my writing groups, we discussed the idea of creating a "themed" anthology.

One of the members lampooned, "It would take a dark and stormy night to get me to write something for an anthology."

A second person agreed, "Dark and stormy night! The world's worst sentence to begin a story is the perfect subject."

Thus the five-minute *Dark and Stormy* anthology was born. I want to thank BlackWyrm experimental fiction publishers for the initial idea.

I also want to give special thanks to the writers for contributing to project, and providing a glimpse into some of the shadows of their minds. Finally I want to thank those who contributed, but do not appear in the book. Thank you to the peer readers, those who helped with book cover ideas and everyone who contributed.

I hope you will join me in suspending your judgment of the "dark and stormy night" cliché' because if you read on I think you will find that the stories are engaging and unique despite a deliberate cliché.

To all of you who do buy and read the book—thank you. If you enjoyed the book, I hope you will take a moment to write a short review.

John W. Smith
Editor

Contents

Advance Praise iii
DEDICATION vii
ACKNOWLEDGEMENT ix
EDITOR'S NOTE xi

I Won 1
    Vittroio T.

Sealed for a Century, and Then 5
    Andrea Doetzel

Master of Disguise 11
    Jacob I. Bell

Oh! How I Wish This Had Been a Dream! 13
    Ed P. De Rousse

Ravine 19
    Luis R Azure

Death Becomes Your Lover 25
    Kat Perry

A Dark Sticky Situation 29
    Jeanette Hammel

A Perfect Night 31
    Sandra Maue

Black on Black 35
    Sandra Kohler Kohlbrecher

A Snowy Saturday Afternoon 39
    Carolyn Mers

The Cemetery Scare 43
    Holly Thieleman

Forever and Always My Love Luna 49
    Nicole Dormeier

Storm Nebula 55
    Mark Laramore

On The Sill in the Night 61
    Gary Adolph

A Grave Too Deep 65
    Charles Schwend

Fairyland Neon Lights 71
    Ellen Carron

Once Upon A Time 75
    Jaime R. 'Jim' Cancio

Unexpected Guest 81
    John W. Smith

About our Contributors 87

About the Editor 99

Other Books by Well Read Press 101

I Won

Vittroio T.

I rose from the ground gasping for air. The distant thunder seemed to move closer with each second. A sharp pain in my chest made me double over. I was sure some ribs were broken. The blood, coming from my busted nose, covered the front of my blouse. My face felt wet. My left eye was swollen shut and the right one was barely open but I could see.

I struggled to my feet and looked around. What happened to me? Where am I? Thunder cracked and lightning streaked across the sky illuminating the town square. The streets were littered with bodies. Cars were overturned and thrown against trees that had been plucked from the ground. Buildings were crumpled. Survivors were struggling to their feet. I saw fear in their eyes as they looked at me.

Did lightning do this? It slowly dawned on me—I had come to the town square to protest the current federal government's policies and I wasn't alone. There must have been eight-hundred of us. We chanted slogans and held our protest signs high as we walked around the square. We were loud and proud. Then I began to hear other voices—opposing us. They mingled with us and began pushing and shoving. I heard shouts of "bigot," "racist," and "homophobe." Soon fists were flying.

Anger and rage consumed me. The next thing I knew I was throwing fireballs at them and at anything else, that got in my way. I called the winds to whip the fires higher and higher; so high that only a downpour could stop them. As I stood watching the all-consuming fire, I passed out.

Where had this power come from? I'm just an ordinary woman who tries to get along with everyone—until I start talking politics. That's when the rage starts building inside me and I want to explode. *Why can't people see what they are doing to this country?* It was then I realized my rage was the source of my power.

Regrets? I have none. For once in my life, I won. I WON!

I was jolted from my reverie by the sound of a car screeching to a halt behind me. Eric, my lover, jumped out of his jeep and ran towards me. He wrapped me in his arms. "Oh, baby, oh, baby! What happened?" he asked.

I burst into tears. He picked me up in one powerful motion and carried me to the jeep. "Hang in there," he said as he raced to the hospital. I could see the police cars and ambulances passing us as we drove down the highway. Eric scooped me from his car and ran into the emergency room yelling for a doctor. I was quickly admitted.

Three days later I came to with IV's dripping into my arms. My ribs and nose had been set and bandaged. The swelling around my eyes had subsided and Eric stood beside me. He looked worried. I tried to smile to make him feel better. *It only hurts when you laugh.* I thought. He told me to stay still so my ribs could heal. That sounded like a great idea. I did as he ordered and fell asleep.

I woke the following day and Eric was still there. I wondered if he would still love me once he found out what I had done at the town square. I tried to speak but he hushed me, telling me that I needed rest. He said that we could talk later. We smiled at each other and a sense of well-being filled me with hope.

We can get through this. I drifted off to sleep again as I heard him whisper, "I'll be right here when you wake up."

The next morning I looked for Eric but he wasn't there. I called for the nurse. "Have you seen Eric the guy who was here yesterday evening?"

"No Miss. I haven't seen him.

As the day wore on, I began to worry. What had happened to him? Out of sheer boredom, I turned on the television. The anchor was talking about an accident—an overturned jeep with no survivors. He said that the jeep was trying to get to the other side of the square but was overrun by angry demonstrators.

I recognized the Eric's jeep. Oh, my God, he's dead. The tears streamed down my face but they were tears of rage. My Eric was gone and they had taken him away from me! *Now they will pay for it.* The rage inside me miraculously healed my eyes, ribs and nose. I bounced out of bed and feeling stronger than ever and raced to the town square. The demonstrators were gone. I stood there shaking; trying to control my rage until I heard sirens and knew I had to leave.

"Good-bye Eric," I said. "Your death will be avenged another day." I released a fireball. It burst in the air and scattered in the wind. *I will return and have my revenge. I will let them forget and relax. I won; they just don't know it yet.*

Sealed for a Century, and Then

Andrea Doetzel

Jake and Marty were cousins, neighbors, and best friends. Their parents shared ownership of a large complex. At 10 and 12 they loved to signal each other with flashlights through their facing second story bedroom windows. Both families shared the chores of property maintenance and grounds keeping for the area along the creek that eventually flowed into the Mississippi River, a mile away.

Their homes were safe on a hill but some of the trails in the woods near the creek were impassable because of backwater flowing in during flood stage on the Mississippi. The flooding kept the boys closer to home and limited their back woods adventures to the tree house, and hunting arrowheads.

One night when an approaching storm signaled its intensity with thunder and lightning Sam, Marty's dog, ran back in the woods along the high trail that followed the creek. Sam sometimes ran away when it stormed, and would go missing for a day or two. Both boys grabbed flashlights and ran after the dog as it began to rain. Their parents were still in the pavilion cleaning up after the evening cookout.

The boys could hear Sam's barking deep in the woods as the soaking rain poured over their shoulders. Briefly, they saw the dog in a flashlight beam as he ran under some brush and disappeared again. Hearing a faint whimpering, they scoured the area and came upon a sloping muddy incline that led to an opening between large boulders at the bottom of a bluff. Calling to Sam, they climbed down and found a dry narrow tunnel leading to a cavern in the hillside.

Sam had gone into the cave and as they cautiously followed, the tunnel led them up a level into an open area. It was a small room with an earthen shelf along the back wall where Sam sat panting in a hollow in the dirt. He seemed at home and safe here, which made the boys, think maybe this was where he came to be away from loud storms. It made sense, since their homes were on top of a ridge where storm noises echoed.

The cave was eerie; all they could hear was the sound of wind in the brush outside the entrance and the distant thunder. In the dim light, they looked around. Jake noticed the glint of something shiny in the corner on the dirt shelf. It was an old mason jar with a rusty cap. As he held it up to the flashlight, it was full of dust but inside they could make out some coins filling the bottom third of the jar. Who had stashed a jar of coins here? They looked at the room closely and noticed that the dirt shelf looked like a bed. Was someone hiding in here?

Putting the jar down, and realizing their danger, they tried to coax Sam to follow them out of the cave. He whimpered then curled up, refusing to move. The flashlights would not last all night so Jake turned his off as they sat together to try and conserve warmth and figure out what to do.

In a shadow, they noticed scratch marks along one wall on a mound of silt. Maybe something tried to dig there. Marty wanted to investigate and break the porous dirt with the jar lid. Jake held the light while Marty scooped lids of dirt to the side. They heard a clink and saw a rusty object about two inches down. An old metal ring could have come from a pair of handcuffs. An escaped prisoner? Near the metal ring, Marty uncovered a ragged strap attached to a pair of boy's overalls. Beneath the strap, they discovered the shoulder and rib bones of a small body.

Marty and Jake remembered their parents passing on a story about a boy that had gone missing years before. The story was from the old man who had sold their parents the property and he swore it was true. The former property owner had grown up there around 1912 and one of his classmates at the one-room school across the road was the Allen boy, age nine, who had disappeared one day after school during a bad storm and was never seen again. He was the oldest of the Allen family children who lived in a shack nearby. His family was poor and he never wore anything but overalls and always went barefoot. With many chores at home, he would sometimes escape and scavenge pop bottles after school, then go right to the filling station to turn them in for refunds. That night it had rained hard and Allen boy never made it home. He was believed to have drowned in a flash flood.

The boys were terrified. Quickly they replaced the soil and moved closer to the dog. Contemplating their fate, they decided to crawl back out, storm or not, toward home. Their parents could help with Sam. They needed two flashlights now as they approached the tunnel and noticed an odd stillness. No brush near the entrance swished in the wind. Marty noticed puddles at the halfway point to the opening and saw brown water seeping slowly toward them.

The entrance was now sealed. It must have been a flash flood that came up further in the lowland and filled the creek up to the bluff and cave entrance. They had seen flooding many times growing up here. It often spoiled their arrowhead hunts along the banks. They knew this water would not recede for weeks because it was spring and rains upstream filled the Mississippi, which, in turn caused their creek to back up. There was no escape and no one knew where they were.

Jake was scared but glad he had Marty with him. Marty was older with some scout training and his dog would protect them from ghosts.

Marty tried to keep calm as an example to his younger friend. They didn't want to panic. An idea for escape was to try to dig out, but a closer look at the dirt, revealed it was in this cave because it had washed in over the years from above through small crevices. It would take all their energy to dig and the grounds over the cave could be underwater flooding the cave if they disturbed the walls.

Marty told Jake they should rest, pray, and remember the good times they shared. Shivering, Jake mentioned he was cold and upset that his new hunting vest, his most prized birthday present, was now all crumpled and damp. It was only a week old and he had worn it every day after school as he hoped to fill the pockets with treasures. Curling close to each other they dozed off, then, one or the other jolted awake only to realize this nightmare was real—there was no way out.

A few hours passed, when suddenly they felt a vibration and noise in the ground. The dog stirred and whimpered as the noise grew louder. It seemed to be coming from several directions. Was it an earthquake or huge waves from the flood crashing against the bluff?

A loud grinding noise disturbed the earth causing rocky debris to fall from the ceiling. They shined one dim flashlight at the ceiling and saw a floodlight emerging with a camera attached and a gloved hand reaching in. They heard a man's voice shouting to others with loudspeakers. A draft of fresh air and light poured into the cave. The men enlarged the hole with picks while one yelled to put the dog in the harness. The rescuer dropped down and fastened the harness first to Sam and then to the transport crate. Sam would be first. Next, Jake was told to put on the harness over his vest and once secured; the helicopter lifted him.

Marty was last and both boys found themselves at the top of a ridge where spotlights moved around their parents and rescue workers waited in the pounding rain. Moving along the road in the emergency vehicle, with their parents beside them and sirens blaring, Jake asked his dad what the beeping noise was that he kept hearing on the radio transmitter.

"That beeping is the built-in GPS device in your hunting vest. It was sewn into the lining and it saved your lives." The boys shared the sad story of the body they found in the cave. They were thankful for Jake's new vest.

Master of Disguise

Jacob I. Bell

Everyone is afraid of something even you. When I was a child, I would lie awake at night, fretting over the oncoming storm. I would hide in the closet and pray for the thunder and pouring rain to stop. Mother never understood my fear of the storm. She said it made me less of a man, just like my father. When Mother wanted to teach me a lesson, she would say, 'come out… come out… wherever you are, or I'll string you up.'

Am I bitter, you ask? We're all chameleons, changing colors to suit our needs. It used to be in my nature to hide, but not anymore.

Now I lie in wait. I'm opening the leather trunk at my feet. What's in there, you wonder? Why, my tools, of course. The first thing I reach for is Zartan, Master of Disguise. The plum, velvet cowl surrounding the Halloween mask is soft to the touch. Black, upside down triangles cover the eyes. I slide the mask over my face. My eyes peek through the holes, bringing Zartan to life. Now I take the coil of wire from the trunk and wrap it around my knuckles. Are you afraid? You should be.

Thunder rolls. The storm is coming. I'm behind you, warm breath echoing through the mask, causing the hair on the back of your neck to stand. The soft beating of raindrops grows harder. It's time for your lesson.

A Dark and Stormy Night: An Anthology

Come out… come out… wherever you are.
I pull the wire taut. It's time to make the rain go away.

Oh! How I Wish This Had Been a Dream!
Ed P. De Rousse

Tap. Tap. Tap. Was all I heard, ever so softy at first. *It's only a dream.* I'll just open my eyes to my familiar bedroom surroundings, then close them and go back to sleep.

I've had bad dreams before. Sometimes I remember them. Sometimes I don't. Lately though, when the bad dreams come it seems all I have to do is tell myself to open my eyes and they go away—never to return. This time will be no different.

I open my eyes and blink a couple of times. It feels like I am awake but I'm never sure until I check my surroundings. First, I must locate the bedroom door. I sleep on my back so that process is not difficult. It just requires a turn of my head to my left.

Just like all the other times, subdued darkness engulfs me. Our bedroom is never in complete darkness because the hallway night-light gives a glow of light to the room. A little light always creeps in, especially since my wife insists we keep the bedroom door open. That subtle lighting makes it easier for me to orient my mind to the surroundings as I wake from one of those dreams.

Once I find the bedroom door, my eyes adjust and my mind begins analyzing the surroundings. First, it locates the bathroom door across the hallway. Searching, I see my wife's dresser and the window. Once I locate the window my mind nudges me awake enough to recognize that I am in my own home and no longer in the land of make believe.

But something is different this time. Those noises that woke me haven't stopped.

What was I hearing and where are they coming from? I turn to look at my wife. Is she breathing? I can see her chest moving. I take comfort in that.

I don't want to wake her. No sense alarming her now. I roll onto my back, take a deep breath, and hold it. I need to be sure it wasn't my own breathing I heard.

Tap. Tap. Tap.

"What is that noise?" I whisper. "It doesn't sound like someone trying to break in. I'll lie here a little longer and try to decipher the source of the sound. Sounds like a dog. *It can't be. Sandy died last year.* I know I heard a dog bark.

My brain always functions at a diminished capacity when awakened in the middle of the night. I take in another breath and hold it. I have to be certain I am hearing those noises and not dreaming them.

TAP! TAP! TAP!

"Okay. That's real—I am not dreaming." I whisper. "I really do have to check it out now."

As quietly as I can, I slide out from between the bed sheets and place first one foot then the other on the floor. I sit on the edge of the bed for a while to insure my brain can function well enough to handle foot movement.

Now where'd that noise come from? I'll check the family room. If it is someone trying to break in, it won't be from the front of the house—too much light. It is during times like this that I appreciate our ranch style house. Not a whole lot of corners to negotiate in the middle of the night when I'm not fully mental. I'll walk down the hallway to the kitchen, turn right, and walk about ten steps to the family room. I can do that in my sleep. No problem.

Walking down the hallway, I hear a different noise. It sounds like someone scratching on a window. It's coming from the family room I think.

I must be still dreaming. That scratching sounds just like something I'd hear in a scary movie.

As I enter the family room, I can feel my heart beating faster. If this is a dream I'm in, it's about to turn creepier. What am I gonna' see when I look out that window? Will I be staring back at the face of some predator peeking in the window to see if anyone is home? Perhaps it's that Jason character.

I wish my mind wouldn't do that. Especially on missions like this.

Now is the time to gather up all the courage I can muster.

A flash of light suddenly fills the window pane. My heart jumps into my throat. Was that the face of Jason I saw in that flash of light?

How come I never noticed that lightening before? Come on now, Ed, just because you saw "Friday the 13th" last night doesn't mean Jason is real. This has to be a dream.

"Get yourself together," I say to myself.

I press my face against the windowpane to get a better look at what is outside. A longer look this time reveals a different eerie scene. The moon is absent in the night sky.

The clouds look heavy and ominous. The wind is gusting. The trees appear to be stretching their limbs in a 45-degree angle. I can hear drops of water splatting against the window screen.

The good news is, I see no Jason, or anything human, animal, or monster. It's just a bad storm so, obviously, I'm not dreaming.

Off in the distance, I see a faint lightning bolt. Suddenly, I hear what sounds like fingernails scraping across a chalkboard.

The thought momentarily crept back in. Jason?

Another look; I see the same moonless sky and tree branches still bending in the gusting wind. I can't see the source of the scratching, though. That means a trip outside to get a closer look. I grab my raincoat from the closet, find my old pair of slip-on shoes, and head out to the back porch and into the chilly air.

There it is again—scratching … and the tapping … and the sound of a dog barking, perhaps more of a whimper.

Without thinking, I search for the spot where I buried our dog.

I buried Sandy out there last year. Is she still in her grave?

Chez, Ed. What's the matter with you? I know it's the day after Halloween, but this is stupid.

Another flash of light. A little closer this time, every hair on my body feels charged with electricity. My body is tingling. Is it from the anticipation of what I fear may be coming in the next few seconds?

Another brief splash of light reveals that nothing has changed. There is still no moon. Those clouds are still huge ominous puffs in the sky. The raindrops aren't as big as I thought, though. There are just millions of them hitting the ground. It looks like a lake out here. The raindrops appear to be coming straight down like the blade of a guillotine. The words "It was a dark and stormy night" pop into my mind. Is this what the author of those words wants his readers to feel?

There are those noises again.

The metal shed in the back yard. That must be the source of the scratchy sound. Standing on the edge of the porch didn't help me see it. I stick my uncovered head out from under the cover of the porch and look toward the shed.

Another flash of lightening!

Ow. Ow. Ow. *Why didn't I think about how much a million drops of rain hitting my head would hurt?*

The brief look gives me enough of an opportunity to survey the terrain. The large oak tree next to the shed is now covering the metal building. What a relief that is. I don't have to deal with it until daylight. Case solved. But what about that barking dog? Why is it barking?

Reluctantly, I pull my raincoat tighter and head out into the rain. The water from my newly formed lake covers my shoes. My pajama bottoms immediately stick to my legs. The rain pelts my head. It feels like a swarm of bees is stinging me. Undaunted, I go on to the sound of the barking dog.

What happens next is totally unexpected and unwanted.

The dog, a stray I've never seen before, works itself free from the fallen branches and scampers off.

I should be happy about that. Not me. I had risked my life, limb, and the threat of Jason to see what was happening here. After all, I just went through; it would be nice to tell the story of how I heroically rescued a wounded animal in the middle of a dangerous thunderstorm.

Now all I have to look forward to is going back into the house to give my wife some plausible story as to why I'm so wet.

Oh! How I wish this had been a dream. It would have been more rewarding.

Ravine

Luis R Azure

It was a bright and sunny day. At supper that night, I wondered why there were no houses in the ravine at the end of our subdivision even though there were houses all around it. Dad said, "Cuz, it's cheaper for developers to build on flat or gently sloping land than it is to get into a ravine and make it flat enough to build. The ravine had probably not changed in a long time." *Good thing.* I thought.

The ravine was thick with trees and bushes on the slope down to the creek. In the morning, if you looked way up to the end of the ravine, you could make out the shape of the rocks at the top looking like the head of a craggy old Indian. I liked the ravine the way it was.

That's where my friend Emery and me built a fort. If you don't think eight-year -olds can build good, you shoulda seen our fort. We used scrap timber from the houses going up on the new street behind ours. Our fort was strong and we covered it with branches that we cut from the underbrush by the creek. We called the creek Wild Horse Canyon Creek. Em and me, we would double dare each other to see how far we could jump across and get safe to the other side without landing in the water. Em was just a high-energy guy and I was the one who usually went home with wet shoes.

Dirt bikers had made some trails on the slopes. There were big old trees on the ridge before the ravine, and a couple on the way down. Our favorite was an old oak, about half way down the slope to the creek. It took five or six kids, hand to hand in a circle to get all the way around it. Em and I had hammered boards into the trunk so we could climb up to the branches. Once high in the tree, we would tie a rope from one of the big branches and then swing out into the ravine and jump onto the trail.

When we finished setting up the fort, we thought it would be cool to camp out in it that night. Mom said 'No, no, absolutely no.' Emery's mom said it would be okay if we could get his grown-up Uncle Josh to stay with us. But Uncle Josh was going to the stock car races. No help there. Didn't matter, we hatched a plan—wait 'til everyone had gone to bed and then sneak out, bringing a blanket, a flashlight and some candy bars.

It takes a long time for grown-ups to go to bed and sound like they're asleep. While I was waiting for them to fall asleep, I fell asleep too. Just a moment later, I heard someone tapping at my window and Scout growled. It was Em. I got my blanket and supplies; Scout whined when he saw I was going out, but I told him to stay and he did.

The eastern sky still held a few stars and a sliver of a moon, but it looked like the sky above us was covering up with clouds. We got setup in the fort and Em wanted to see what it was like to swing on the rope at night. He got to swinging out real good and made the jump to where I could hear him land, but couldn't see him. I went down the trail to find him. He stayed still in the bushes, jumped out at me in an ambush, and scared me good. That was the easy scare of the night. There is more to come—believe me.

Just about then, the skies opened up. First, the rain was soft—then it got strong and it was almost like being in a carwash without a car. We couldn't see a lot except water and the shape of the big old oak. It looked like part of the tree was coming at us. Em saw it too, and we huddled together. Something was moving our way. Hard to see in the rain but it looked like a man, near naked, a big man, and now he was standing in front of us. His skin was like bark, and his eyes were dark, way in, like the way a tree heals over a branch that is cut, with a hood over the cut part.

He had a small pouch by which he carried on his waist. I tried to touch it and see if it was real. I nearly fell over reaching for it. He jumped when I tried to poke it, laughed and spat, and then he turned to me. I was gonna say, 'don't hurt us mister', but I couldn't move my tongue or lips. Then I hear Em's voice, higher than usual. He managed to wave and say, 'Howdy, Mister.' Em was always my most positive thinking friend.

The tree man kept staring. "I'm looking for an innocent." He leaned toward me and asked, "Are you an innocent?"

I wasn't for sure what he meant, so I asked him the same way our old teacher, Miss Henrietta 'Bucktooth' Stormant did when we were wisecracking. "Exactly what do you mean by that Mister?" That was the wrong answer.

He turned toward Em. "Are you an innocent?"

Em said, "I guess so; at least that's what my Aunt Laney must think, and she's a judge. She calls people guilty all the time, and she never called me that. So I guess I must be innocent." That was the right answer. He told us he was bound up in the tree for many moons and could only come out when it was dark, stormy and rainy. I guess that's why he looked so *barky*. A long time ago, he was the last of his tribe that lived by the ravine. He was hanged there by five men. They wanted his land, the last land held by his people. When they hanged him he cursed them real bad, but his ancient curse meant that if he had done any bad wrongs himself the curse had to include him. He got locked into the tree and couldn't come out 'til an *innocent* would do him five favors.

"Will you perform five acts of innocence and free me?" he asked Em.

"Sure, Mister."

That's just Em's attitude, can-do and will-do. He told Em the first two acts. Take down the rope we used for swinging into the ravine and remove the boards in the tree we used as a ladder. Em looked at me like, would I help him? I nodded.

Then the tree man said, "I will teach you the rites for how you will accomplish the other three tomorrow at sunset. You must be alone." He looked hard at me. "These ceremonies must be accomplished after dark and before sunrise." He kind of saluted Em, and started to fade back into the tree just as the rain was letting up.

We headed for home through the gloom. My folks had already done a look-see in my room. I guess Scout kept whining and got their attention. I got it big time when I got there. Grounded for two weeks, my bike was put on the ceiling rack in the garage, and I had to take up chores my sister usually did. Mom said I would have time for them cuz I wasn't going anywhere. I don't know what Em's folks did. He wouldn't say. I for sure don't know how he got back out there the next evening. But he did, and he wouldn't talk about that either.

Em seemed to be changed by it. We were still friends and we sometimes walked together in the ravine. I always kept an eye out on that tree, but it didn't seem to worry Em at all. We didn't climb in it anymore. Emery was a more serious person now. He stayed that way the whole school year. He made good grades like always but he wasn't so easy to know anymore.

The ravine is still there, the old oak, and the creek are all pretty much the same. That next winter we had a hard freeze all the way through spring. The rocks up at the end of the canyon must of froze, cracked and crumbled right out of their Indian shape. By spring, they just looked like a pile of rocks. You couldn't make anything out of it. Looking up the ravine wasn't the same.

Dad said that he believes nothing stays the same; everything changes if you wait long enough. I guess that is all what started the night Em and me met up with the tree man. After all, what could a kid expect—it had been a dark and stormy night.

Death Becomes Your Lover

Kat Perry

One dark and stormy night, my lover ventured out
in hopes that he could claim his prize
and turn his luck about.
He thought that if he spoke the words,
confessed his love for me
that I could then be with him, that I could be set "free".
And so with lovesick valor, he came
knocking at our door
believing he could stand to hide his love for me no more.
Imagine my great horror when I saw that it was him;
that he was the dark stranger whom my husband
motioned in.
Now shaking in our parlor, his clothes all soaking, wet
his voice began to tremble, his words I'll not forget.
"I've come for my beloved.
Her heart belongs to me!"
"You've no right now to keep her here,
you have to set her free!"
My mouth went dry as cotton, my stomach tied in knots.
Had he forgotten all our plans?

Our dreams?
Our schemes? Our plots?
My husband, he was wealthy, I'd no intent to leave …
At least not without my fair share, of that you can believe.
How foolish of my lover, to think I would choose him!
Confusing feelings of true love
with those of carnal sin!
I quickly gained composure and took my husband's arm
preparing now to offer up the best of all my charm.
"Of whom are you now speaking, Sir?
I don't believe we've met …"
"You poor thing, you must be confused
My God! You're soaking wet!"
My husband's eyes were glaring; his face had turned bright red.
"You've come to claim my wife? I see …
I'd sooner see her dead!"
With that, he'd pulled a pistol from just inside his coat
first pointed at my lover and then against my throat.
I do remember crying and begging for my life …
of pleading with my husband,
"How could you? I'm your wife!"
My lover's desperation soon overcame his fears
but attempts to try and take the gun took
my remaining years.

The moral of my story, so tragic, don't you see?
Take heed of all your actions or you'll share
a fate like me.
It only takes one moment to take away your life
when Death becomes your lover on
a dark and stormy night.

A Dark Sticky Situation

Jeanette Hammel

It was a damp and dreary evening, but Theodore 'Ted E.' Bear was not going to let that stop him. It was *Trunk or Treat* night.

It used to be called *Trick or Treat* night. Kiddies wore costumes and went house-to-house saying "trick or treat" as neighbors opened their doors to them. The idea was that if they didn't get treats, the kids played tricks. Some of the tricks were not nice. Things like placing buggies on shed roofs or dumping outhouses in the yard.

The newer, safer way to go trick or treating is to go to your local church or other safe places where the adults keep their decorated car trunks open and filled with treats. Everyone wears costumes, has a great evening and takes home enough candy to last for months. Almost. Dads have been known to snitch a Snicker or two.

Theodore Bear admired the big grizzlies and so that is how he dressed. Mother had also made a big bag for his candy and treats. While she sewed his costume and bag, she baked cupcakes to give to her callers.

Theodore met his friends and they walked to the church together. It was safer walking together should they come upon some bullies or the evil, sinister Professor Foznoggle. He was a known candy thief.

All went well and they had a good time until it was—TIME TO GO HOME.

Theodore thought he saw a shadow lurking around the corner. All he could think of was that shifty, beady-eyed candy thief, Professor Foznoggle.

His little friends walked faster and faster. Thank goodness, it was a short walk home. He felt like he was running in slow motion.

The sinister shadowy thing ran faster too ... UNTIL unbeknownst to Theodore, his bag tore at the corner. He was leaving a trail of caramels, banana chewies, grape gummies and a chocolate bar or two. The last to fall through the hole was one of his mother's cupcakes.

The runner behind them got slower and slower due to the sticky candy gunk on his shoe soles.

It became silent except for Theodore 'Ted E.' Bear and his friends, for you see, the shadowy, beady-eyed, shifty follower stopped to eat the cupcake and then, "POOF," he DISAPPEARED! For mother's secret ingredient was EVAPORATED MILK.

A Perfect Night

Sandra Maue

The wind howled like the pain of a wounded animal. Bullets of water exploded on the window glass. Angry streaks of lightening punctured the sky followed by earth shaking booms of thunder.

Nights like these were perfect for relaxing in a big chair, next to a roaring fire, with a soft lap blanket, a sifter of brandy and a good ghost story to read. Jameson took a sip of his brandy and sighed with contentment before returning the glass to the end table.

He lifted the heavy book and continued his reading, the symphony of the storm complimenting the story as it unraveled before his eyes.

A good while later, thoroughly engrossed in his book, Jameson became distracted by the odd flickering of the fire. He pulled his attention away from the words on the page to focus on the flames. He could have sworn they reached out of the fireplace, stretching toward him. The flames burned a steady yellow, orange, and red, dancing within the confines of the fireplace. He took another sip of brandy then chuckled.

"You're spooking yourself, boy." He said to the empty room. He took a third sip of the smooth, golden liquid before returning the glass to the table. Listening to the raging storm, he settled deeper into the chair before dropping his eyes to the pages in his lap, losing himself in the tale of menacing spirits.

Many pages later, Jameson was again, distracted by the fire. This time, when he turned his attention to the flames they bent towards him, reaching their hot fingers towards his legs. Astonished, he watched as they stretched longer and longer, inching closer to the lap blanket. He noticed, with surprise, that he felt no heat.

A strange mist slithered into the room from the fireplace, gliding over the heatless flames, as if it had been hiding there. Waiting.

The grey vapors flowed into the room to swirl into a shapeless blob directly in front of him. Slivers of ice cut across his skin but whether from the mist or bone freezing fear he wasn't sure.

His hands began to shake as the mist shifted and flowed into a form, slowly at first, taking on shape and substance until a beautiful young woman floated before him. An angelic face, framed by long flowing light hair, a slender neck and a voluptuous body hovered a few feet from him.

Jameson's mouth dropped to his chest. When he tried to speak, he couldn't manage the barest of whispers—his throat dry as dust. Unwilling to take his eyes from the haunting beauty, he blindly reached for his brandy, knocking the glass to the floor where it shattered. He did not look away.

His numb brain dimly registered the fingers of flame receding back into the fireplace. Swallowing hard, Jameson felt his constricted throat muscles relax. He swallowed again.

With great effort, he forced words past his numb tongue, through chattering teeth.

"Who are you?" he croaked. The beautiful woman's smile was warm and tender. She stretched her arms toward Jameson, inviting him into her embrace.

He began to rise, reaching for the angel, never taking his gaze from her soft eyes. The tips of his fingers were inches from her when the woman's face began to change.

The bones and flesh slid down the skull like melting wax. Her mouth thinned to reveal sharp pointed teeth dripping with slime. Her eyes fell into her skull leaving empty black holes. The silken hair disintegrated, melting into stringy greasy strands that hung in clumps. The fingers of her delicate hands stretched into gnarled, boney sticks tipped with jagged claws. Her flowing gown decayed to rags barely covering her shriveled skin.

The hag opened its hideous maw and let out a howl that made Jameson's blood run the wrong way. He fell back into his chair letting out a howl of his own.

The creature opened its mouth so wide that the face disappeared. The creature's teeth were as long as Jameson's fingers. He screamed.

It lunged toward him, howling. At the same time, the fiery fingers shot out of the fireplace to rip at the top of his foot, biting hard and deep.

Clawed hands thrust into his chest, grabbing his heart, squeezing the life from the throbbing muscle. Jameson jolted out the chair, a wheezing, breathy scream exploded from his body. His clutching hands reached for the creature only to grasp empty air.

His breath labored, heart thundering in his chest, he cast once again, reaching for the creature. The room was empty.

The book and blanket lay crumpled on the floor. His foot throbbed. He looked at the fire nervously only to find cheerful, flickering flames. Reaching for his brandy, he spotted the shattered glass on the floor.

He collapsed back in the chair. Running a shaking hand over his clammy face, a nervous laugh escaped his lips. Though the ferocity of the storm had lessened, the wind howled down the chimney.

"Yep," he said, with another laugh, "a perfect night."

Black on Black

Sandra Kohler Kohlbrecher

The forest was a lush green as the dense, morning haze rolled in. The dew glistened with rays of sunlight filtering through the trees.

It was a quiet time, with only a pair of mourning doves cooing in the distance.

All of a sudden, the sleeping forest began to rumble. In unison, the horrified birds flocked together as they flew towards the sky. The kingdom animals scurried back and forth, as the rumbling noise approached with a fierceness they had ever heard.

Having left the King's castle, with his lord's order, the Black Knight came roaring through the forest at lightning speed. His lord's order: kill the great fire breathing Wyvern dragon, just beyond the forest.

There was no time to spare, for the dragon had been seen in the woods. The Villeins were in dire need.

Having extinguished their candles and fires by nightfall, their huts lay dark. Their stillness sent eeriness among them, like the quiet before a storm. Through the night, they could hear the monstrous dragon's stomping as he roamed nearby. His fire-breathing roar lit the sky a blood red.

With morning on the rise, their prayers had been answered. They had made it through another night of anguish. They too now heard the approaching sound. Was a storm of doom heading toward their village? As everyone came out of their huts, they gathered alongside the dirt roads. Glancing in wonder at one another, they kept their ears alert.

Like thunder from above, the noise grew louder. Before their senses could adapt to what was happening, the great Black Knight on his twenty-hand steed, cane galloping at lightning speed through their village. The dust, like a massive cyclone, encircled their bodies.

The Knight's enormous black steed, adorned with reins of silver and bit of gold, his long black mane flowed in the wind. His master upon him in armor so bright the Villeins feared loss of their sight. His massive sword hung from one side as his shield the other. Before they knew, he was gone.

With a trail of dust left behind, their silence broke.

"He came to save us … our village. The Black Knight will slay the Dragon of Fire. We will no longer live in fear of darkness. He will set us free."

As the dust settled, the Villeins gave thanks by making the sign of the cross.

Knowing the dragon slept days from his roaming nights of terror, their days were normal. This day would not find that to be.

Their prayers continued as hours passed. The roars started once again only now there was a difference. They were of screeching, deafening pain, until they heard no more. Once frightened by the dragon's roars they were now frightened by his silence. It had been a long, tiring day. Had their great Knight slain the Dragon of Fire?

Did their Knight succumb to death? They believed in their lord as well as their beloved knight.

They had no choice but to wait.

Before day's end, the Villeins saw their Black Knight returning Once again, they lined the roads. His great steed carrying not only its master, but towing as well the head of the once fire menacing Dragon of Fire.

With sunset close, the Black Knight ventured onward. Now secure in their huts with candles and fires ablaze.

No longer did they fear their nights.

A Snowy Saturday Afternoon

Carolyn Mers

It was a typical Saturday afternoon at our house; Dad was in his reclining chair watching some college football game, a glass of Pepsi on the table by his side. We had all learned at an early age that this meant "Do Not Disturb." He savored his afternoon football games and he didn't give them up for anyone or anything, nor did he care to share or include anyone in his passion. I think he enjoyed the solitude.

My younger brothers Bobby and Johnny were in their bedroom playing video games. They were obsessed with manipulating a chomping face around a maze, which was gobbling up various colored dots. They could spend hours batting a fake tennis ball back and forth with their controllers, while listening to the likes of Kiss and Led Zeppelin.

Mom was in the kitchen, preparing a bounty of food for stocking the deep freeze in the garage. Every week she prepared several meals at once in order to keep the freezer stocked and to make the weeknight meal preparations easier. Today there was beef stew slow simmering in the crockpot, a huge pot of spaghetti on one of the back burners of the stove, and on another burner was a big skillet of sloppy Joes. Some of the sloppy Joes would be today's dinner, with the leftovers going into the freezer.

From my room I could smell the aroma of the chocolate chip cookies in the oven. My hair up in large three-inch brush rollers, I was painting my nails, listening to my newest Elvis album, while talking on the phone with my friend Janet. We were making plans to go roller-skating that evening.

This is how we spent every Saturday afternoon at our house, and Janet and I went skating every Saturday evening. I'm not sure why we had to spend an hour on the phone planning and discussing it.

But, today seemed different. The weatherman had forecast a major blizzard for our area. He said to be prepared for the snowstorm of the century. The heavy wet snow had already been falling for a couple of hours, but none of us seemed too concerned. We were all so wrapped up in our own little lives that we didn't give the prediction any attention. That is, until the electricity flickered a few times, and the phone went dead. We each had to look out our respective windows to see what was going on. It was a beautiful winter wonderland outside.

We all came together to look out the living room window and marvel at how much snow had already accumulated. Making sure the scene was the same in the backyard, we all went to look out back from the kitchen window. We could see the power lines drooping low from the weight of the snow, and swaying from the gusting wind. Dad set about gathering up the flashlights. He headed out to the garage to get his battery-operated lantern that we used for camping.

Mom had already begun to pull out the candles and matches. Dad said that those power lines were not going to hold up much longer. This time the weatherman got it right.

As Dad came back in the house with the lantern, we could hear the buzzing and popping as the line outback snapped from the pole. It was suddenly very quiet, no cheering from the football game on TV, no bleeping of the tennis ball bouncing from the video game and no Elvis singing "Love Me Tender." There wasn't a sound anywhere, it was pin-drop quiet … kind of nice.

Dad told the boys they needed to get their boots on and start shoveling the front sidewalk. But Mom said everyone needed to eat first. It was a good thing she had already started frying up the French fries and everything was ready to eat. It was so quiet while we ate; you could hear the chewing. We weren't big talkers; we really didn't have much to say to each other. When we were finished eating we threw our paper plates in the trash, and we all started to bundle up to head outside. Mom warned the boys to stay in the front yard and away from the power lines. I grabbed three large plastic bowls so I could gather up some of the fresh snow for making snow ice cream later. I wanted to make sure I had gotten good clean snow before the boys trampled over it.

We all pitched in to help shovel the sidewalks and clean the snow from the cars. After scraping the walkways and cleaning the cars, we built a snowman together. It was the biggest one we had ever made because Dad was so tall, he could make it as tall as he was. We even had a snowball fight. It was fun to watch my parents laughing and acting like kids in the bright moonlight reflecting off the snow.

We went in and changed into warm dry clothes, all of us had chosen the warmth of flannel PJs. After all, we weren't expecting any company on a night like this.

I proceeded to add milk, sugar and vanilla into my bowls of snow, the boys stirred until it was mixed thoroughly. Then it was divided into smaller bowls for each of us. While we were enjoying our rare treat of snow ice cream, along with Mom's freshly baked chocolate chip cookies Mom pulled out the Monopoly game and asked, "Who wants to play?"

Everyone in unison said, "I do!" Including Dad, who never played games with us. We were enjoying our family game night by lantern light, when there was a knock on the door. I went to see who could possibly be out in this weather. It was my friend Janet. She gave me a puzzled look and said, "You're not ready! Aren't we going skating?" I turned and looked towards the dining room and saw my family laughing and enjoying being together.

I looked back at Janet, and said, "No, I don't think so, I am having fun here, besides I doubt if the roller rink is even open." She turned around and walked away. I closed the door and returned to the game and my family.

The Cemetery Scare

Holly Thieleman

"It was a dark and stormy night. The thick fog covered the cemetery like pea soup."

"Oh not that old thing again Henry, give it a rest already. You say this every time All Hallows Eve rolls around."

"What Victoria? It's the best time of year to say that phrase. I mean, just look." He pointed to his left at the thick grayish white fog. "See? Every time we come up to see the world—fog."

"Alright, alright: You win. I'm just sick of hearing it year after year for the past three hundred years." She rolled her eyes placing her hands on her hips.

"Victoria, have I ever told you that you look lovely in that old tattered and torn Victorian dress of yours?" Henry flashed a smile.

Her white eyes narrowed at him as she pursed her lips. "Really Henry—do you think that you can butter me up with saying how pretty I am in the dress I was buried in?"

"Well ... I just thought," he swallowed.

"Thought what?" Victoria's face softened some.

"Well, it's just that we get one night a year to have fun. And I just thought that I'd tell you how lovely you look." He paused for a moment. "But when we come up from our graves right as the sun goes down on this night we always see vandalism take place and we never do anything about it." He ran a hand right through his head as if running his fingers through his hair.

Victoria nodded knowing that Henry was right, but she wasn't in the mood for scaring people—even to stop them from committing vandalism or any crime for that matter.

"You know Victoria, I feel like scaring the living this year. You know, as a way to teach them a lesson."

"But we've never scared the living before," she pouted.

"Well, let's scare them, then. I'm tired of not being able to be seen or heard on this night."

"Well … what do you have in mind?"

"You run and scream while I chase you as if I'm going to kill you. It will scare just about anyone that comes in the cemetery for whatever wrongful purpose they have planned."

Victoria's eyes widened a little. "I don't know Henry. That doesn't sound like a good idea to me. I'd rather the living's law men handle it."

Henry looked in the distance and saw two teenagers dressed up for Halloween walk through the cemetery entrance. One was wearing a Frankenstein mask and the other was wearing a Michael Myers mask from *Halloween.* "Here come some vandals, Victoria. Please? Please will you help me scare them?"

Victoria sighed then nodded. "Alright, but this is the last favor I will ever do for you." She took in a deep breath and let out a scream that was louder than the thunder rolling in. One of the teens looked around the cemetery a little freaked out wondering what he just heard.

"H ... Hey ... did you hear that?" the teen in the Michael Myers mask asked, his voice in a quiver.

"No, I didn't hear anything, Brad."

"Dude, I can barely understand you. Take your mask off."

Brad removed his mask and stared at his friend. "I heard something over there, Derek. Like a shriek, or shout, or scream, or something."

"Of course you did," Derek replied after removing his Frankenstein mask and rolling his eyes. "You claim to be a "werewolf" with those super sensitive ears of yours. Seriously B, cool it with the werewolf shit. It's so old now. Besides, it could be the wind or thunder from the storm, you ninny."

"D, I'm not joking this time. Besides, I only say that to mess with your sister. You know how easy it is to scare her." Brad replied narrowing his eyes some.

"Oh, sure. This coming from the pansy who screams at the sight of the tiniest spider."

Brad shuddered at the mention of spiders. "Hey! You try having one land on your fucking face ready to attack, then come talk to me about being afraid. They're evil I tell you. EVIL!"

Derek removed his backpack from his shoulders and unzipped it. He grabbed two cans of spray paint. "Uh huh. Yeah, sure. Whatever you say, now are you just gonna stand there, or are you gonna help me spray paint some graves? Unless you're too much of a pussy to do it?"

Brad blinked before making a disgusted face. "Why must you always say that about me when I don't want to get in trouble with the law? Besides, I told your sister I would make sure you wouldn't do anything stupid." He stood in front of Derek; mask in hand, arms stretched out in protest. Lightning crashed behind Brad illuminating him like those stars portraying angels in movies and TV.

Derek snapped. "Shut up you pussy! Kelly was the one that wanted us to get along better for her sake, since you two are an item now!"

Brad cringed every time Derek called him derogatory names.

He spun to his right; he heard a loud shriek and a maniacal laugh over the top of more thunder. "Please tell me you heard that."

"I ... I did." Derek stood swallowing hard before walking towards the laugh and shriek.

"I told you! I told you I heard something! But did you believe me? No!" Brad shouted raising his arms again.

"SHHHHH! Do you want us to get caught? Maybe just some other local pricks trying to scare us. Ye ...Yeah. That's gotta be it."

Brad and Derek were almost in each other's' arms from the loud crash of thunder and the brightness of the lightning. Victoria floated towards them a little bit, wailing again. They both turned around quickly to see if anyone or anything was behind them ... there wasn't. Derek turned back to the direction they were walking and almost brought Brad down with him. There standing before him was Victoria screaming and wailing, not even two feet away from their faces.

"You can't escape from me!" Henry shouted behind her.

"HELP ME!" Victoria wailed. "HE'S TRYING TO KILL ME!"

Derek and Brad looked at each other screaming at the top of their lungs before bolting back the way they came. As they ran, Henry caught up behind them shouting "I'LL KILL YOU!" while trying to grab the boys by their costumes.

Derek and Brad ran like a cheetah clocking its prey, just to get out of the cemetery while screaming their heads off, almost like the whistling of a tea kettle.

"I'M NEVER COMING TO A CEMETERY EVER AGAIN!" Brad shrieked making it back to Derek's house. Henry and Victoria had never seen the living run this fast before. Once they reached the entrance to the cemetery, both of them laughed so hard that their heads almost came off their bodies.

"Henry that was the most fun I've had in my three hundred years of death. You sure know how to make them scream."

Henry's laughing slowed as he floated back to his grave as more thunder boomed and lightning crashed. "Ah, yes it was. I don't think I've ever seen anyone scream like a little girl in forever. So what say you on doing this again for next year?"

Victoria nodded yawning. "I say yes. How we scared them was the best thing we've ever done. I like scaring wrong doers now, especially during a storm. We should get the rest of our grave mates in on this."

"I agree Victoria. I will say that this night was the perfect time for a cemetery scare."

Forever and Always My Love Luna

Nicole Dormeier

Dear Journal:

Some days all I can think about is dying in some way, whether by accident or on purpose—dying in a way that I can be remembered. I know this may be depressing, but I'm not the only one who feels this way. You see—I have cancer. Some days I don't want to have to go through the pain any more. I don't want to have to deal with the heartache of leaving so many people behind. But it's inevitable. I can't help that I was the chosen one to carry this curse. That I am the one on the worst rollercoaster ride of my life.

I had cancer when I was five years old. I made it, but the doctor said that it would likely come back. I didn't want to believe it, but my worst nightmare has come true. My cancer came back—with a vengeance, I was not prepared for.

When I was first diagnosed with cancer, I lived day to day. I didn't worry about my future. My parents made me do things constantly but when the doctor said, I was cancer free, my face lit up with pure joy. From that day on, I thought about what I wanted to be when I got older. I decided where I wanted to go to college. I was able to attend school with other kids, not just stay home and have my mom teach me.

I made friends, although only two stayed with me through thick and thin. I never told them about my diagnosis and remission. If they saw one of my scars, I would make up a lie to tell them, rather than the truth. I didn't want them to know and I didn't want to be treated differently. All I wanted to be was a normal kid.

It's sad that now, even in high school, my best friend Katie still doesn't know. Neither does my boyfriend Jason. I still don't want to tell them, but I know that sometime soon I will need to. Telling them this secret will be one of the hardest and most life changing things I could possibly do. Why have I been silent so long? I'm afraid they will be mad at me; that they won't want to stay my friends. But I need to take my chances.

... And my chances were closer than I thought...
~ Luna

Many things could happen on a dark and stormy night. For instance, you could have the usual things that go into these sorts of writings such as werewolves or vampires hanging around. Or you could have a midnight kiss and a dance in the rain, or even giving birth because some people do that, too!

Well, I'm not as lucky as these people are. Granted, hanging out with a werewolf or having a vampire hanging around isn't something most people would want. If I had a choice, I would choose the vampire or the werewolf over what I found out last night.

✶✶✶

Feeling pain shooting from my hip to my foot I screamed out. My boyfriend Jason had just dropped me off at home after a day of running errands. My parents had stopped him on his way out. That's when he heard me scream. He ran back with my parents just behind him.

"Luna what's wrong? What hurts Angel?" *I don't know why he calls me Angel when my name means moon.* Jason knelt down next to my bed. I couldn't speak or make any noise except another piercing scream.

"We need to take her to the ER Paul," my mother said with such calmness in her voice that even I was shocked. "I'll get the bag and you go get the car ready. Jason, pick her up and get her in the car as fast as you can."

"What's going on?" he asked, confusion taking over his words. I let another piercing scream rip from my throat. "Why is she doing this?"

My mother never answered him. She went to the closet and got the big duffel bag that hangs on the back of the door.

"She never told you, did she?" she asked with a somber expression.

"Never told me what?" Picking me up, he carried me out of the room behind my mom. I clung to his jacket so tight that my knuckles were white.

The rain pelted the windshield with such force that my father was having trouble seeing the road. I heard tires squealing but I couldn't tell him to slow down.

Reaching the hospital in record time, the car became silent. I had just let out three screams while Jason stared at me forlornly. I had heard him ask my mom questions, only for her to shoot them down. She wanted me to be the one who told him about my condition. I was placed on a gurney and carted away. A nurse stopped my parents and Jason from going any farther. I saw my father grab hold of Jason's arms and pull him back.

It took an hour for the doctors to do all the tests. I was taken to one of the single patient rooms, where I fell asleep instantly. They had given me an oxygen tank and some hard-core medicine to dull the pain and steady my breathing.

There was a constant beep next to me and all I wanted to do was yank it out of the wall. The door opened and papers rustled. I didn't even attempt to open my eyes. The nurse walked over to the bed and checked all the machines. The door opened once more. "Are we allowed to come in?" It was my mother.

"She's sleeping but you may come in for a little while." I could hear the smallest hint of a smile in her tone. Something warm took hold of my too cold hands. Realizing it was my mother, I squeezed. I cracked open my eyes and my mother's face came into view. She was smiling at me.

"Hey honey, how are you feeling?" She rubbed my forearm absentmindedly.

"I'm holding on. It's my worst fear right?" I couldn't even look at her when she answered.

"Yes...the cancer has come back." She stopped rubbing my arm and squeezed it. "You need to tell them."

"I know mom...I just don't want anything to happen. Is Jason still here?"

"Yeah ... he's pretty shaken up about this whole thing. Your dad and I didn't tell him anything." Her voice low, almost a whisper. "He broke a chair." I laughed just imagining him getting mad and throwing a chair at the wall.

"Will you go get him?" I asked after I could breathe once again.

"Yeah." My mother got up, kissed me on the head and walked out the door. Seconds later, Jason busted through the door. Eyes puffy from crying, he shut the door and walked over to the bed. I didn't want him to see me like this, but I couldn't help it.

"Angel, what's going on? No one would tell me anything." He plopped down in the chair next to my bed.

"Okay... I've been keeping a secret from you." I whispered the words, not looking at him. He stayed silent. "When I was really little I had cancer." When he didn't say anything I looked at him. He had tears rolling down his cheeks cutting marks into his perfection. Lifting a hand, I put it up to his cheek and wiped away the tears.

"Has ... has it ... come back?" I nod my head yes and watch him break down. "How bad is it?"

"I don't know. All I know is that it has come back." I felt a tear roll down my own cheek.

"Why is this happening to you? You already had cancer, you don't need it again!" Jason grabbed hold of my hands and squeezed.

"I know, I know. I never wanted you to know I had cancer when I was younger, but somehow I knew that one day I would have to ... and now that day has come." All I could do was whisper. "Whatever happens, always know that I love you."

Dear Journal,

She died...I got three amazing months with the girl I love and then she was taken from me. I wish I had married her, but that didn't happen. I will never forget the love of my life.

Forever and Always Luna My Love,
Jason

Storm Nebula

Mark Laramore

It was as dark as night when Joe awoke to sounds of thunder, as if from a faraway storm. Despite the complete darkness, he recognized the intimate surroundings of Pasha's cabin. Nestled in the center of the starship, along with the other crew cabins, it was protected from accidental decompression by additional bulkheads and passageways to each side.

Joe eased himself up from the bed, careful not to disturb Pasha. She was swaddled from head to toe in blankets. It was cold in the room. He felt his way blindly to the hatch. It was not hard to find in the darkness, he knew this cabin nearly as well as his own. He moved into the passageway, where the thunder was louder, and he was greeted by quick and intense flashes of light from the portholes that lined the opposite side of the passageway, each flash accompanied by the sound of thunder. He gazed through the nearest porthole, and realized his predicament.

The ship floated in a dark, colorful nebula. Deep blue, purple, and red gasses swirled and eddied around the ship. Charged particles sweeping past moved along by the stellar currents of some unseen star, reacted with the hull to create arcs of lightning every few seconds. There was no atmosphere outside the ship to carry the sound of lightning crashing, but inside Joe heard the thunderous reverberation of the hull from where the electrical arcs contacted it at both ends. Though louder than it had been within Pasha's cabin, the sound was muted even as the lightning arced just centimeters from the porthole.

Flashes of blue-white light from the arcing bolts were the only source of illumination along the entire corridor. The ship was without power, and Joe knew that it was only a matter of time before it would be out of air. There was no way to tell how long that might take. He had no idea how long he had been sleeping. The boiling storm of the nebula had killed the engines and knocked out the power—but how long ago?. He turned, and made his way toward the back of the ship, to see if he could restart the flow of power.

In the engine room, a glowing form rushed toward him out of the darkness. He was too startled to move as the engineer let out a silent scream and swung a large wrench at Joe's face. Joe flinched and raised his arms protectively. The spectral wrench passed harmlessly through his body, and the engineer faded away with a grimace of fear and pain on his face.

"What the...?" Joe's unfinished question trailed off, the last word fading like the ghost who had just assaulted him. He was not sure he had recognized the ghostly image, but memory tugged at him. Fear took hold before the memory could, and Joe turned away from the deeper darkness that shrouded the depths of the engine room. He needed light before he could bring himself to delve any further.

He made his way forward, past Pasha's cabin, where he paused to listen. Hearing nothing, he continued past his own cabin, and headed toward the storage lockers near the bridge. Flashlights would be stored there along with weapons and EVA suits. He hoped that he would not need either one but thought he might secure a sidearm just in case.

A dark figure blocked his way just meters from his destination.

"Joooeee." The voice was low and moaning, and Joe wasn't sure if it was a question, or a statement.

"Why, Joe?" The voice intoned. There was no doubt that this was a question. The voice seemed to gain strength, and the dark figure became more cohesive, even though neither Joe nor the figure in front of him had moved. He recognized the specter, but could not remember the name. Memory was such a fragile thing.

"The nebula knocked out our power." Joe answered, "We must've ended up here because Pasha never completed our flight path before...."

The dark figure dissolved in front of him, and Joe never completed his thought as he watched the apparition disappear entirely between two bright flashes of lightning, as if it were a shadow—an illusion dispelled by the sudden illumination. He was not sure what he had intended to say. Why had Pasha not finished the flight path? Her job as navigator was to make sure that the ship travelled the interstellar lanes without incident. Joe had always thought of her as dedicated and uniquely qualified for her job. He had other concerns now, however, and turned back to his task.

The storage lockers lined each side of the corridor and one was open. Joe hesitated before reaching into the open locker. The bridge hatch was open as well, and Joe noticed light and movement on the bridge. He moved through the open hatch and saw that the light came from the control panel in front of the Captain's chair. The Captain sat there, his head and hat protruding above the back of the chair and silhouetted by the light of the console.

As the Captain swiveled around in his chair, Joe realized that the light was not coming from the console but rather from the Captain himself. A ragged crater of flesh and bone dominated half of the Captain's face. His cheek and left eye were gone. A flap of skin hung down along the side of his nose, and covered half of his mouth. Blood was flowing down his neck from the gaping wound. His uniform was soaked with blood.

"Get off of my bridge." The hanging flap of skin made a smacking sound against his lips as the Captain spoke. He raised an accusatory finger and pointed at Joe as he spat the last word. "Murderer!"

Memory flooded back. Joe remembered walking through the open hatch before. How long ago? He could not remember. He shook his head and pushed the memory away. It was too terrible.

"No!" He shouted back at the Captain. "No!" he yelled as he turned and fled back to Pasha's cabin. "No, no, no!" He continued to scream as he bent over her desiccated corpse, carefully wrapped in the bed sheets that now served as a shroud.

Joe could no longer contain his repressed memories. He had walked onto the bridge and found Pasha with the Captain. When she should have been charting their course, she was engaged passionately with him. Joe knew that Pasha and he were not exclusive. All four, male crewmembers shared her intimacy. That is the way it had always been with Pasha. He had never witnessed her with any of the others before. They had always had the decency to keep it in the crew cabins, and at some point, he had come to think of her as his own, and had fallen in love.

He wanted to believe it was a jealous rage that had overtaken him. That he had committed his crimes without malice or forethought. He remembered the cold feeling in his gut, however, as he had turned slowly and deliberately. He remembered ice in his heart as he opened the storage locker, retrieved the gun, and methodically began to re-load.

✯✯✯

He even remembered laughing as he returned to the bridge and leveled the gun at the Captain. The Captain wheeled at him a split second before Joe pulled the trigger and the slug missed its mark. Pasha was thrown back from the impact. She died instantly when the bullet pierced her heart. Her body fell against the Captain's console and engaged the star drive, sending them hurtling through space with incomplete navigation data.

He had flown into a rage then, not from jealousy, but from his own actions. His next shot found the proper target, striking the Captain in his face. He had killed Smitty next, the gentle scientist who had been his best friend in the crew, after Pasha. The hapless man had come up behind him to see what was going on as Joe still raging, shot him.

Cold and calculating, he turned his attention to the engineer. The chief engineer had heard the shots, and armed himself with the only weapon he had available, a big, heavy wrench. He had charged Joe as he entered the engine room, but Joe put him down before he could even get close to him.

Outside, the stellar winds continued to push against the nebula, finally herding the gas cloud away from the starship. No longer wracked by arcs of lightning, the ship emerged from the storm. Lights slowly flickered on as the engines restarted automatically. The power was restored.

Joe looked away from Pasha and stared at the corpse in the chair next to the bed. He barely recognized his own face, dried and leathery from decades floating airless in the nebula. Now that he remembered his own slow death by suffocation, his consciousness, trapped by the nebula itself for all these years, finally faded into oblivion.

On The Sill in the Night

Gary Adolph

As I sat upon the windowsill
that dark and stormy night,
I tried to think what drew me there
to turn out every light.

The clouds hung low and heavy
that dark and stormy night,
shadows moved across the lawn
in fashions just not right.

Thunder shook my little ledge
that dark and stormy night,
lightning flashed across the sky
revealing just below
a site to cause me fright.

I didn't dare to breathe up there
that dark and stormy night,
for fear that what I saw below
would be impressed upon my sight?

They moved so slowly, inch by inch
that dark and stormy night,
the iridescent trail they made

glowed shiny, silver bright.

Slimy slugs were all about
that dark and stormy night,
head to tail they crawled about
interlocked and holding tight.

Determined now they ably moved
that dark and stormy night,
up the vine draped trellis and the
downspout gutter pipe.

Quickly to the cupboard did I run
that dark and stormy night,
it was an arsenal that I searched for
and Morton Salt that I did spy.

Like waterfalls I poured on them
that dark and stormy night,
then slowly did I see them melt away
as I turned on the light.

It was a grotesque site below me
that dark and stormy night,
globules of salt and slime
dripped from every leaf and vine.

I returned to sit upon the sill
that dark and stormy night,
every light that I could find

Gary Adolph

was on and burning bright
and they are burning still.

A Grave Too Deep

Charles Schwend

Dark, ominous clouds boiled overhead, obscuring the grey cast moon, heavy with electricity and threatening a torrential downpour. The air was crisp and bone chilling. The wind screamed through the pines like an Irish Banshee, forewarning the gravedigger, Dugley Deep, of a pending horror. Digging at the bottom of an unfinished grave changed the way sounds were heard. Down there, the wind-driven, thrashing pine limbs produced a moaning sound. Dugley, ever diligent, was wary of the ominous presence he felt.

A clawing scratch came from Dugley's spade as he thrust the steel blade, polished from digging many graves, forcibly down through the hard, unbroken, gritty soil. He was far from finished with his task. Needing the necessary depth of six feet, six inches, the last measurement was only four foot and five inches. Only his head was above ground level. If one could view the rotating head, it could be thought a bodiless head was spinning around possessed—a headless corpse.

Broken ground flew up from the hole, landing in a heap to be used as back fill after the coffin was lowered and the vault lid sealed onto a concrete box. A ladder was positioned at one end of the deepening rectangular hole, an escape route, up the ladder and through the maze of mostly upright stones to arrive at his truck in the least amount of time. His rusty old pickup was in dire need of a tune-up. The tires were near bald and had prevented driving up close onto the damp grass. To try a speedy escape would be pointless and result in spinning tires on the slippery vegetation, then capture in what surely would be a horror scene.

He thought he could hear someone calling out his name. Dugley stopped digging to focus his hearing. A quick look around did not relieve his apprehension. A shiver coursed through his body as he sidled up to the mantel lantern. He was comforted by its warming glow. The lantern was battling the heavy darkness closing in, and seemed to be losing. Picking it up, he gently shook the light and smiled reassuringly, hearing the fuel slosh. Anxious to finish his job, a quick measure of depth proved disappointing. It was only five feet deep. It will take another hour or more of digging before he could go home. *The deeper you get the harder the digging*, he thought.

A coyote howled in the distance, answered by a nearby barking dog. Murmuring surrounded Dugley, forcing another check of his surroundings. A mist fell onto his face. Looking up he saw a large opening in the cloud cover directly above. There were no night birds flying. No tree limbs to hide creatures of the night or to obscure his view of the sky. Where did that moisture come from?

Dugley trembled, remembering stories told of people recording voices from the cemetery graves. Some recordings were made during séances to locate important papers, treasures or identities of a spirit's murderer. Other stories revolved around 'dousers' identifying unmarked grave occupants and their gender. Dugley did not believe in superstition, but always avoided tempting the spirits. He did not walk on occupied graves and always spoke in a reverent voice when working at the cemetery.

The spade struck something metallic. How can that be? This is undisturbed ground. His body stiff with apprehension—a brain freeze weakened his thinking as he methodically dug around the struck object. Sparks flew as the spade struck the object again. Prying the metal up with the spade brought an ancient looking sword to the surface of the grave floor. A purple aura surrounded it. A shiny surface reflected the lantern light and there was no oxidation of the metal or deterioration of the handle's rough finish.

Dugley knew from his readings that sharkskin was used for making sword handles because the sandpaper-like surface would secure the sword in a man's hand, made slippery with blood during combat. But sharkskin, no matter how tanned or preserved, would not stand up to being buried in damp ground for decades. Picking up the sword produced a rather unpleasant tingling that ran up his arm and across his chest, stopping at his heart. A heated flush flowed over his body, then changed to a deep chill.

He heard crying but there was no one there. Looking around he noticed a marble angel, part of a headstone standing three graves down. Did he see tears making dark lines run down her face? His body tried to continue in its mechanical chore of digging, when the ground gave way to a subterranean opening. Dugley landed on all fours, disoriented and in pain.

Looking up through the grave opening made the hole look small. He could not estimate the distance due to the lack of light. The lantern did not penetrate this deep and made but a glow.

A singing came from what appeared to be a long tunnel, not high enough to allow upright walking but maneuverable if he kept hunched over. Feeling his way along the shallow tunnel Dugley approached a lit cavern with no evidence of a light source. It seemed the air just glowed. Small gnome-like people were cavorting in what appeared to be a tavern of sorts. Scantily clothed maidens teased and flirted while serving mugs of beer to groups of little, wrinkled, aged men.

The servers did not rebuff attention from the little men, but were laughing and giggling as they banged the large drafts on the roughly made tables. The small men were dressed in muddy-brown and emerald-green clothing. Their faces were deeply etched, eyes sparkled with delight and all had heavy beards. Their skin tone was dark, belying their existence underground. Cautiously inching forward and using the heavy sword like a cane, Dugley entered the cavern. A shout from the boisterous group caused the merriment to stop. A rush of red- nosed, bearded, miniature people surged in his direction. He held up the sword in a defensive gesture.

As the moving sword sparkled in the light, the wee men and servers stopped and kneeled down in front of him, heads bowed. They acknowledged his presence in words he did not understand. Lowering the sword, Dugley stared at the blade and noticed an inscription written in a strange script.

An older, frail-looking man stood and slowly approached Dugley, his hands raised in a peaceful gesture. He carefully studied the sword. With a non-threatening expression, he straightened himself, reaching his full height. The old man began to speak in a voice Dugley understood. "Who are you? How did you acquire our Sword of Wrath? Where did you get it? How did you get here?"

The apparent leader of the group was still mouthing words when Dugley interrupted him. "I was digging a grave, above, when I found this sword buried and then fell through into the tunnel behind me. Please tell me that this is all a dream."

"What is your name?"

"Dugley Deep".

"Dugley Deep. This is no dream. We are the Igen-nouts that fight the Denizens of the Underground."

"Denizens of the Underground? Who are they?"

"They are the soul suckers of those buried above. We can hold them off, but only the Sword of Wrath can kill them. Many centuries ago, they stole the sword, but could not destroy it. They hid it from us thinking they could maneuver around our defenses. Ancient legends tell of the sword's return. Now, please give it to me."

"How do I know that what you are telling me is the truth?" The heated flush filled Dugley. A feeling of purpose and honor overcame him. A hissing, clicking and scratching sound echoed ever louder, through the tunnel behind him. The small people ran back in fear, and started setting up a barricade across the cavern entrance.

"The sword ... the sword. Use the sword. It's the only thing that can kill them. Quick, turn around and strike them down."

Turning, Dugley could now see in the darkness with

clarity. Huge spiders, with blood red eyes and grinding mandibles filled the tunnel. The swinging sword struck down the nearest spider and was quickly replaced by another. Raging combat continued for hours without help from the tunnel dwellers who hid behind their barricade. When the last spider was cut down a roar of acclaim echoed through the tunnel. "Now everyone is safe," said Dugley.

"No. That was just a small patrol trying to locate us. Now do you believe we are the true owners of the sword?"

"Yes. Here, take the sword." Handing over his found treasure, Dugley's world turned dark.

Dugley woke with a knot on his head. The adjacent grave had given way and the coffin lay in pieces around him—the skeleton lay across him. The fallen ground had nearly covered him and he gripped a long pointed root in his hand.

Fairyland Neon Lights

Ellen Carron

My name is Malissa Francois, born in Louisiana in the early fifties. As I grew up, I didn't have much opportunity to see or learn about the outside world. My world was a houseboat, which belonged to my Grannie and Papa, where we drifted from one swamp to the other. Sometimes the boredom and confinement would be almost unbearable. So, I would close my eyes and daydream about leaving the swamps in search of a "fairyland".

There were special occasions when Papa would come home and tell Grannie and me to put our best dresses on because he was taking us to the big city. I would get so excited that it was hard to contain myself.

Going to the city meant looking at pretty clothes, watching fancy cars drive by, and eating ice cream and cotton candy. The most exciting and fascinating time of the trip, though, was in the evening when we strolled under the blinking, flickering, bouncing neon lights. They were so beautiful. I felt as though I was walking in an enchanted palace of bubbling colors, and I would think to myself, *This is what I want. Someday I will to live in this wonderland.*

On my eighteenth birthday, I announced to Grannie and Papa that I was moving to the city. It broke Grannies heart, but there was no talking me out of my decision.

Finally, the day came, at five o'clock in the morning Papa, Grannie and I boarded a rowboat and headed for the city.

After a long trip through the swamps to the Blood River and over Lake Ponchatrain, we reached our destination. I remember climbing out of the boat and standing on the dock in the red coat Grannie had made me. She gave me a hug and Papa just stood in the boat showing no emotion. As they rowed away, I felt sadness seeing Grannie wave goodbye with one hand and wiping tears from her eyes with the other. But the anticipation of my new adventure in the city and living under the neon lights dismissed all the sadness.

As the rowboat disappeared into the misty fog, I turned and started walking in the direction of the hotel. Crossing the street at the curb, I felt a sharp blow to the top of my head. Waking up sometime later, my suitcase had been disarranged and my money stolen.

Staggering to my feet, still in a daze, I found myself sitting on a park bench. My mind was racing with fear. Burying my head in my hands, I began to cry hysterically. For the first time in my life, I was alone, cold, and broke. As I sat on the park bench, trying to decide what to do, a voice behind me yelled, "Are you okay?" And there was a handsome man, standing at the curb leaning against a fancy car. He yelled again. "Is there something I can do to help?" Coming over to the bench, he seemed concerned. His voice was so kind and gentle that I told him my story. He offered to let me stay at his place as long as I needed. I felt it was okay to get into the car with him.

He introduced himself as Brian Swartz. He kept reassuring me not to be afraid and that I was safe. He also began to talk about his business, which was arranging appointments for lonely men to be entertained by pretty ladies.

Over the next several months, I fell deeply in love with Brian and would do anything he asked to keep his love. I forgot the morals my Granny and Papa had taught me. I became a prostitute. My existence was in turmoil; filled with unhappiness and regrets. After several years of walking under the neon lights, my life turned into a series of dark and stormy nights; my fairyland fantasy had disappeared—a piercing reminder of the little innocent swamp girl who sat on the banister of the houseboat not having a care in the world. One night reality hit me, the way I was living was wrong; I had made so many mistakes. I wondered if there was a chance to go back home.

The chance came when Brian disappeared. His "Lady of the Night" business folded. I was free again. Immediately I packed my things and went to the docks. There I met an old man who agreed to take me home for a fee. Jumping in his boat, we proceeded on our long journey over the lake and up the river. It seemed to take forever to reach the swamps but finally, we were there. As we rowed through the channels, I sat back in bewilderment, at the wonderland before my eyes.

There were beautiful colored wild flowers nestled in blankets of greenery, with moss draped cypress trees and birds of every species. It was a heavenly sight to see and my eyes filled with tears. I couldn't help feeling alive. When we rounded the last bend in the channel, I caught sight of

Grannie and Papa. They were on the porch of the houseboat. Papa was fishing and Grannie was sitting in her rocking chair knitting. As we rowed closer, they looked up and Grannie recognized me. She jumped to her feet as I stepped on the houseboat and they met me with hugs and tears. Granny and Papa welcomed me home and I knew that I was forgiven for leaving them for the city.

After supper, I went outside and sat on the banister as I had done years before. Listening to the sounds of frogs croaking and the hoots of an owl a short distance away, I had forgotten how comforting the swamp sounds had been when I was a child. I watched the blinking and flickering fireflies as the old excitement rose in my chest. Suddenly it occurred to me that my fairyland of neon lights was right here in the swamps and on the houseboat. My dark and stormy nights of the past were gone.

Once Upon A Time

Jaime R. 'Jim' Cancio

There comes a time when the truth comes out; the problem is—will you recognize it? Sometimes the truth is hidden and dies with the people that know it. I always liked the way the Spanish said it, "First the Devil knows your name—the Devil has a very long memory."[1] It is this that best be known, "There comes a time, with the Devil in your heart and soul, God turns his back on you."[2] The Devil always knows the truth.

I am the last to know the truth, and for what I know and all the dead people behind me, the Devil will soon welcome me. You think you know the truth but you don't—you have been lied to all these years. I am a contract killer, professional, a specialist in the services I perform. When my work is finished, I walk away and no one knows that the person or persons I killed were murdered. At other times it is obvious it was a murder. I am paid very well for my work and do whatever pleases my employer.

My employer at the time was a Saudi prince; my price to him was $750,000 in 1968 U.S.D., paid up-front, prior to the assassination—success or failure. Pay-offs and expenses were also provided. A thing like this is a once in a lifetime job and

---

[1] Quotes from *The Devil's Linoera*
[2] Quote from *Pan's Labyrinth,* 2006 DVD writer and director Gulllermo del Toro.

if you manage to pull it off, you will never be able to provide your services again. The Saudi prince had held a grudge that dated back to 1948 from a visit to Palestine and Israel where he had been rebuffed and humiliated in front of his family and his nation. The public rebuke festered, growing each year until at last, the wound ruptured with a desire for retribution—with fatal consequences.

In this type of assassination, there is always a patsy. We found one in Los Angeles, an immigrant harboring hatred for all that had happened to him. All we had to do was channel the hatred for Jews in the direction we wanted him to go; drugs, alcohol, and feeding his appetite for little boys brought him around. We fed his hatred; provided him training and practice and more drugs, and of course the weapon. With a hit like this there is no chance he will be able to make a get-a-way but we don't tell him that. We never tell him that the assassin is killed at the location of the murder.

There are two firearms used in this attempt and they both must appear as the same weapon. To do that takes money and the skills of a master gunsmith. One weapon was a semi-auto Walther TP®, manufactured in 1964 in caliber 22 Long Rifle [six shots semi-auto pistol]. The other was an Iver Johnson Cadet® 55-A revolver also in 22 LR [eight shot revolver]. Both their barrels were removed and two new barrels were made using a brand new barrel blank. A new barrel reamer was used to have identical rifling land and groves. For the TP, a barrel was cut to exactly two and 7/8 inches and one end was threaded to mount a sonic silencer.[3]

---

[3] Normal barrel length is 2 3/8's inches.

This device converts the sound of a discharge by boosting to a sound frequency human hearing cannot detect. Both barrel sections are configured for their respective firearm and both barrels are "blued" to match the finish on the firearms. Two new firing pins are machined with the striker heads of both firing pins rendered to the correct length. Both firing pins are then ground down using a specific location on the grinder wheel to provide identical tooling marks. In any forensic examination of the ammo fired from either gun it will appear to have been fired from the same gun.

The TP's rebound spring has been cut down to use subsonic 22 Longs and the silencer renders the discharge truly silent. That gun with a spent shell deflector and collector is completely hidden within the pistol grip of a Bolex H16 Reflex Movie Camera mounting an Angeniux 12-120 mm zoom lens. In other words, the gun looks like a camera. It is but isn't. The aperture adjustment equipment has been removed. The void is filled with the end of the barrel and silencer of the TP. When the trigger of the gun is depressed the camera starts running—when fully depressed the gun will fire semi-automatically. Anyone looking at the camera will see it as a camera and the film can be processed, if need be. What is not obvious is that the viewing ground glass lens has a set of crossed hairs etched into the glass in the middle of the frame lines. The gun has been precisely adjusted to hit the point-of-aim at six feet.

The Saudi prince demands guaranteed success. The TP's ammo is coated with a mixture of fecal matter and rancid garlic painted over using boat varnish that contains arsenic. Doctors treating a gunshot wound will never suspect the other agents. The first shot will be into the head of the target, just behind mid-center of the right ear to penetrate the skull, reach the spinal column and destroy the brain stem and cerebellum. The wounded brain will be assaulted by four different mechanisms with no way to survive. One shot one kill—guaranteed. If it doesn't kill outright, it is only a matter of time.

All the details had been worked out—location, date and approximate time verified. Weeks earlier, the Saudi prince, traveling with his favorite wife and four children, came to me in Boston wanting to renegotiate my contract. He wanted to double my fee. He was afraid someone on the assassination team might get caught and that the investigation might lead to him. He wants me to kill every member of the team after the assassination.

When the man at the top worries the Dominos, start to fall. At the end of the Dominos, it will be my turn.

With reservations, I accept his deal. Mentally I start making my own plans to deal with the prince. He will only pay after everyone is dead which could also mean I would never get paid.

Two Days Later

The Saudi prince goes to Washington, D.C. leaving his family in Boston. I step in and kidnap his wife and children. Contacting the Saudi prince, I tell him my reservations and make it clear the only way he will ever see his wife and children will be after the money is in my hands. He has no choice. When he gives me the money in cash, I will let him retrieve his family.

Just after midnight, the 5th of June 1968, at the Ambassador Hotel in Los Angeles, California, the assassination was performed and a 42-year-old presidential candidate of the United States was shot three times, two by the pasty and once by me. I missed the mark but managed to get the bullet into the right ear. He died early the next morning. Five others were wounded that night. The patsy got caught; no problem he thinks it is all his idea. Later that night Helen Esteridge, a woman in a polka dot brown dress, was killed but no one will find her. After being tied up, a sock with a 1.5-inch ball bearing was shoved down her throat and then her mouth was taped over. Her body was dumped in a drain hole in an abandoned business district alleyway in Century City. Her body was tied to 100 pounds of lead. She isn't going anywhere and she won't be found.

Bill Spence, who stood next to her at the hotel, also died that morning, left floating in nitric acid. Others followed but not before the money in the envelopes I gave them were back in my hands.

The Saudi prince was very pleased. In Boston, he brought me another $750,000. I left and called him on the telephone in his hotel room telling him where to find his wife and children. In this business, if you can't trust someone you don't last very long. In the dark shadows, I waited for him.

The prince drove up outside the warehouse and searched until he found an unlocked door. He immediately went to his seated wife surrounded by her bound daughters. He worked on the knots that bound her arms to the chair and then loosened the ties on her feet. When he lifted her, he never noticed the trip wires attached to the belt of her dress. The trip wire set off three grenades. I went to the bodies, stripped them of jewelry and took her purse and his wallet that contained twenty-five $500 bills and thirteen $50 bills. When I searched his car I found half a million dollars, six bags of diamonds and a dozen gold bars in his attaché case. The trouble with guys at the top who get nervous—the dominos always fall—but not this domino. I put a permanent stop to *his* way of thinking and picked up a 'little extra cash" at the same time.

Works for me.

Unexpected Guest

John W. Smith

Brian moved to the lonely stretch of beach in order to watch the sunset and the stars appear in the night sky. He wasn't a day person. He enjoyed being alone and found life in the city and in small towns bothersome. In both, people were always sticking their noses in other people's business—his business.

He found The California Lost Coast along the cliffs of northern California on a drive last summer. It was a drive to nowhere in particular but there it was; the perfect mix of privacy and a sea view. Contractors hollowed out the side of the mountain, constructing a two thousand square foot fortress of solitude. Three bedrooms, two baths, and all the amenities he could think of, including a series of thick, sliding glass doors that allowed him to step onto his expansive deck that faced the ocean.

His first two nights had been sheer heaven. He made an early dinner, sat on the deck and watched the sunset. He slowly enjoyed his meal and a glass of red wine. After the sun had dropped below the horizon line of the Pacific Ocean, he stared into the sky and watched the stars reflecting on the water.

Later, when the chill of the ocean air forced him indoors, he sat in front of his computer and wrote. He was a writer of short stories, two novels and the occasional play. His current book, a novel about a recluse was in the final stages after five years of revisions. Life was perfect.

He smiled as he thought of his friends who kept trying to fix him up. They kept saying 'All you need is a woman Brian. Someone to care for you."

He wondered what woman would want to live in a cave, and how the lawyers would split the side of a mountain in a property settlement. He laughed. If he needed companionship, he could go to town and find company, then come home alone—and happy. He didn't need complications.

Brian took a break from the computer and looked out his window. The stars had gone out. The full moon glowed in hazy dullness as it crept over the cliff above.

Behind that hazy moon was darkness blacker than the inside of a coal mine at midnight. Grabbing his binoculars, Brian walked out on the deck and began searching the sky. What he saw and what his mind was willing to accept were two different things.

Black clouds rolled toward the coast. As they moved closer to shore, the stars disappeared. The moon's light was absorbed into the front of the clouds. It was as if the sky was being folded in.

Tendrils of massive grey-black clouds floated in front of the darkness, which grew with each passing minute. It sucked the light from the night sky. *What is happening?* Brian thought as he watched the encroachment of the black vacuous harbinger. It was making its way to the beach—to his home.

The wind howled chasing in the expanding waves. Each wave slammed against the cliff as if to tear it to pieces. Each successive wave was higher and more brutal than the next.

The storm was now less than a mile from the coast. It was time to batten down—Brian moved the table and chairs inside. He looked at the three-inch -thick steel-framed doors and windows. Would they hold back what was surely coming?

The first drop of rain struck his deck as the clouds passed over the cliff. He watched as sheets of rain smashed and slashed the glass of his deck doors. The doors seemed to bow in the wind. The sound was deafening.

The waves now pounding the cliff only inches below made the house shudder. Sick with fear he wondered if his underground garage was flooded. Why hadn't he done what the contractor suggested and built the garage on higher ground? His underground garage could be his escape. The doors had been fitted with watertight seals but he had no confidence in them.

He walked back to the deck windows. If the wind blew them in, he would be crushed by their weight. He wanted to go to a safer part of the house, shut the doors and ignore the howling wind and the waves. There was no "safer part" so he resisted the urge to run. He had to watch this test of the structure he had designed.

The storm continued. It had been three hours since landfall. The radio reported wide spread damage at least fifteen miles inland. There was flooding, homes destroyed, and people missing. He felt sorry for the people who had been hurt or killed or had lost everything, yet, he felt a sense of pride welling up within him—he was safe and dry. His house had survived.

As if the sea was intent on taking from him all that he had, a huge wave scaled the cliff face and washed over his deck with unimaginable force. It slammed against the heavy glass doors.

He heard a thud and looked out. Something was struggling, caught between the vertical posts of the deck. It tried to pull itself up, but it was trapped. A second wave reached up and covered whatever it was. It took several seconds for the water to clear.

Brian saw a giant fish. It had to be shark or some other giant from the sea. He was amazed that the waves had lifted it so high.

A third wave struck the windows but they held. Walking to the sliding door, he watched the water drain and fall back into the ocean. He realized that what he had seen was not a fish at all but a woman.

She must have been on a boat or diving when the storm hit and had been carried by the current and thrown by the waves to *his* deck. *How can she be alive?*

Another wave struck the deck. She continued her struggle, attempting to free herself. Lightening flashed. Brian realized that if she freed herself, she would fall onto the rocks below and be crushed by the waves.

Her scream jolted him into action. Opening the sliding glass doors, he grabbed her around the waist and pulled with all his might. At last, she was safely inside and the doors were once again closed. Covering her with towels and blankets, he laid her on the couch. She was shivering violently. As she became more lucid, he gave her some wine to calm her.

She continued to shiver. Her wet suit provided no protection from the ocean storm and the frigid water. The two stared wide-eyed out the windows as the storm continued on its deadly journey east.

Hours later, the clouds began to clear. The moon was just beginning to set on the western horizon; stars reflected off the ocean and life began to return to normal. The waves remained high, but everything appeared safe. Brian's 'cliff house' survived the storm of the century without damage.

Wrapped in blankets, the woman curled up on the couch, her legs tucked beneath her. She accepted another glass of wine as Brian began to make her some food.

He knelt in front of her. "You are safe here. I will take you home when the roads clear. Until then, please rest and regain your strength."

She smiled, ate, but said nothing. The next morning he found her wrapped in the blanket standing on the deck. The two of them watched the now calm ocean. It no longer beat upon the cliff face. The solitude had returned. Brian was at peace. Not only had his home stood untarnished against the storm, but he had met a companion that intrigued him.

"Please, let me call your family, I am sure they are worried about you. I will take you home."

Again, she smiled, and dropped the blanket. She was naked and beautiful.

"What happened to your diving suit?" Brian muttered looking into the living room for the wet suit. "You must get dressed."

She smiled. Holding his cheeks between her palms, she kissed him—hard and urgent. Her kiss sent shock waves through his body. He was about to speak when once again she looked out over the ocean and leaped over the railing falling to the rocks below.

Brian screamed as she gracefully dropped towards the rocks and Pacific Ocean. She hit the water with knifelike precision. There was barely a splash. Seconds later, she surfaced. She wiped her blonde hair from her face and looked up. Waving, she slid head first into the water, her giant tail fin flipped into the air as she began her journey home.

Brian stared out towards horizon. He smiled as he considered his first house guest. No one would believe him if he told them he had been visited by a mermaid on a dark and stormy night. It didn't matter. He only hoped that she would return. Until then, she would be an interesting tale for one of his magazines.

About our Contributors

Gary Adolph

Gary resides in Highland, Illinois, and is a 32-year associate of Wal-Mart Stores. He is a confessed bibliophile and has a passion for poetry, early science fiction, nature, and adventure books.

He has been writing poetry since high school. Mr. Norman Jackson, a high school English teacher in Farmington, Mo., nurtured his love of literature. He finds satisfaction in seeing his boys acquire a collection of great books and his desire is to pass on that love of reading to his grandchildren and instill that love in children of all ages through poetry and prose.

With the continued encouragement of his wife Cindy, he created a storybook around his poem, *I Like To Read*, through Mix Book. He was able to share that journey with his granddaughter's school class and provide a copy for their library. He has since created another book, *Reflections*, that is a collection of some of his favorite original poems.

Louis R. Azure

Bearing an all too common surname, the author created a persona and the appellation listed above. He graduated Lake-Hill Academy of Arts and Sciences when he was seventeen and made sporadic attempts to attend classes in botany at Smoke Rise University in Weebentoken, New

About the Contributors

Jersey. While there, he was a member of the Garden State Dirty Hands Society.

In the late 60s he was implicated in the Chess Pie scandal in SE Pennsylvania and had to flee with only the clothes on his back and a large wheel of cheese. Broke and discouraged in New Orleans he lived off the cheese for a time then worked as a short-order cook, dockhand, broker for the high-end horseradish trade, and translator for the small but militant Native American nation of the Boalousehbeauxm headquartered in Vidalia, Louisiana. After their extinction, he migrated upriver and settled in America's prosperous breadbasket, never to be hungry again.

He is currently working on projects related to men's issues and a soon to be nascent TV series with a working title of You *Ain't Got Scratch*. He likes scathing letters to the editor(s), enjoys writing reviews of restaurants, movies, telenovelas, and agrarian reform efforts. Generally, he prefers fantasy to reality.

Andrea Doetzel (Pen Name)

Andrea started writing poetry in grade school. Her uncle, a famous poet, encouraged her through the years. She has had many of her writings published and has been featured in columns of local newspapers and magazines in the Midwest.

Her first book was published in the fall of 2013 and is entitled *Meet Me in the Meadow*. Now retired after 23 years in the insurance industry, she lives on a friend's farm in rural Illinois enjoying the peace of country life. She is currently a member of The Highland League of Writers group and the members have offered insight and encouragement in her writing ventures. You can contact Andrea at andoetzel@hotmail.com

Jacob I. Bell

Jake Bell has a B.A. in English, as well as an M.A. in Humanities from the University of Louisville. He is a freelance writer whose diverse work ranges from technical writing to fiction. His first short story *The Dragon's Claw*, was published by Wizards of the Coast in the *Dragons of Time* anthology. He is currently writing his first novel, *Lord of the Dogs*.

Jaime R. 'Jim' Cancio

Born in Bakersfield, California Jaime 'Jim' R. Cancio, [the R. is for Rebel], is a retired career management businessman who has been lucky enough to travel to 37 of these United States. He has earned a B.A. in Multi-Media Journalism (2007) and a Certificate of Multi-Media Communications (2010) from California State University, Bakersfield. He is an award winning professional photographer/videographer with journalism experience that dates back to 1962 as a contributing writer and photographer for the *Bakersfield Californian Daily* (TBC) newspaper when he was in high school.

He worked from 1989 to 1996 as a staff photographer and copy editor for the TBC.

Jaime has photographed a wide range of subjects from crime scenes and business conferences to presidents. He has photographed seven United States presidents as well as actors, major government and business personalities, artists and entertainers.

You can contact Jaime through email at jaime_cancio@yahoo.com.

Ellen Carron

Ellen was born in Southeast Missouri. Growing into an adult, she attended Kaskaskia College and later attended Southeastern Louisiana University. She plays the guitar, and writes music. Carron also does free-hand pencil art. Her poetry has been published in her hometown newspaper in Vandalia, Illinois. Writing novels is her primary interest. She now lives in Highland Illinois, where she attends The League of Writers writing group.

Ed P. De Rousse

Edmond P. DeRousse retired as an educator for the Illinois Department of Corrections after twenty years. He served seven years in the United States Army and worked eight years as an executive for the Boy Scouts of America. He earned a B.S. degree in Secondary Education and a M.S. degree in Workforce Education from Southern Illinois University-Carbondale. He likes to tell people he is working on his seventh life. The previous six were youth, college, military, Boy Scouts, finding a new career path, and corrections. The seventh is writer, author, and speaker.

DeRousse is the author of *The Adventures of a Common Man* and *Choice and Consequence / The Adventures of Pete Russey: A common man*. Both are part of his humorous and fictional *Common Man Adventure* series. The books are published by Tate and are available through any on-line book provider and in digital format.

After many adventures of his own, including raising two children, he and his wife of more than forty years have returned to their roots in Southern Illinois.

E-mail Edmond at: common.man1@live.com

Website: http://acommonman.com

Nicole Dormeier

Nicole is a senior at Edwardsville High School where she has dipped her toes into the writing pond with this anthology. She enjoys spending her free time pursuing art including writing, drawing, crocheting, and painting. Her plans include earning a degree in lower elementary education and incorporating art within her daily lesson plans.

Jeanette Hammel

Jeanette was born and reared in Highland, Illinois. She is a great-grand mother to five girls and one boy. They do not live close by. Since she cannot hold them and read to them, she writes stories and sends them copies.

She has published writings, but has based her latest series of stories on teddy bear tales. The adventure stories of Theodore 'Ted E.' Bear and his family. These stories are now being passed onto another generation.

Jeanette did not start writing until later in life. She likes to see others smile or laugh as they read the adventures Ted E. and his friends. Who knows what she will write about

About the Contributors

next. Will it be about the sinister, beady-eyed, Professor Foznoggle or the meek and mild Pheneas Pettybone?

Jeanette enjoys writing children's stories and reads them at every opportunity in the hope that she brings a little joy into the lives of children and adults.

Her motto is "Everyone should do at least one thing each day that makes THEM happy." We know just reading a tale of Theodore 'Ted E.' Bear will do just that. Jeanette is a member of The Highland League of Writers writing group.

Sandra Kohler Kohlbrecker

Sandra is the author of the mystery, *"Graffiti Bridge."* She has published eight short stories along with other writers who belong to the Highland League of Writers in Highland, IL. Their anthology is entitled *Words: An Anthology of Short Stories*, published by Black Rose Writing.

She is currently working on her novel *New Haden*, along with a collection of short stories. When not pursuing her writing, Sandra is fulfilling her many other artistic talents. She lives in her hometown of Highland, IL, with her husband William. You may contact her at bksk22@yahoo.com.

Mark Laramore

Mark is a software engineer living and working in the St. Louis metropolitan area. He and his wife Tamra have raised two wonderful children: Alicia who is the oldest and her younger brother Corwin. Corwin is currently serving in the US Navy.

About the Contributors

Mark's mind is often found exploring the far-flung worlds of the galaxy and the darker recesses of those worlds. He enjoys relating the results of those outings through the medium of the written and spoken word. Mark is a member of the Ocular Voice writers group, and *Storm Nebula* is his first published work.

You can contact Mark at his e-mail address: mark@laramore.net.

Kat Perry

Kat currently resides with her husband and their three children in a small, rural community located in central Illinois.

Besides having the honor of being included in this compilation, she has also had several of her works included in the anthology *Words*. Her poetry has been published in various publications over the years.

Kat is currently working on her first novel and hopes to have a collection of her poetry published in book format.

Sandy Maue

Sandy lives an unassuming life with her family in Illinois. Her greatest joy is being a wife, mother and grandmother—a *young* grandmother. Though she has a professional career, her passion is writing. She has been spinning yarns for many years and is currently working on several projects. Sandy writes in different genres, but her primary focus is writing mysteries.

She is the moderator of the Ocular Voices writers group and is currently working on murder mystery collaboration with some of its members.

A Dark and Stormy Night is her first professional publication. She looks forward to entertaining readers with more of her stories in the future.

Carolyn Mers

Carolyn is a team member of the speakers bureau for the St. Louis chapter of the Alzheimer's Association. She is also a member of the O'Fallon Illinois Writers Guild and a self-employed ceramic artist. Mers is the author of *The Alzheimer's Roller Coaster: The Story of Our Ride*.

Carolyn was born and raised in Cahokia, IL, and is currently living in Belleville. She and her husband Dan have three grown daughters and two grandsons. Throughout their 44-year marriage, Carolyn and her husband have lived in several mid-west states due to Dan's IT career. In 2004, Dan took an early retirement so they could return home to be the supporting partners in the early stages of her mother's battle with Alzheimer.

Carolyn openly shares her story of the first ten years of her mother's illness through speaking at churches, nursing homes, libraries, support groups, book signings, and to anyone who wants to listen. The sequel to *Alzheimer's Roller Coaster* is a work in progress—as the journey continues the ending is yet to be written! Someday in the near future she would like to add romance and historical fiction writing to her resume. You can contact Carolyn by e-mail at cmersarc@charter.net or follow her blog at http://alzheimerrollercoaster.wordpress.com.

Charles 'Chuck' Schwend

Charles is the author of *Dragon Dreams, Words to Read: A Collection of Short Stories, Gulag #7 - The Authorized Biography of Karl Heinz Lawrenz*, and the editor of *Words - An Anthology of Short Writings*. He co-founded the Highland League of Writers in 2008. Charles majored in journalism and has a specialization in Musiology, which is the conservation, preservation and restoration of museum artifacts.

He served twenty years in the U.S. Navy, retiring as a Chief Petty Officer. You can contact Charles at schwendcharles@yahoo.com or visit his website at www.charlesschwend.com.

Vittrorio T. (Pen Name)

I was born under the sign of Scorpio and therefore, very passionate about love, politics, and life especially now in my "golden years." I graduated with a B.A. in Latin American Studies and an M.A. in International studies. I have traveled the world to make what I've read and learned about countries more meaningful. I spent two and a half years teaching English in Japan in the early 70s when the Vietnam War was still raging. I traveled throughout Asia before I returned to America.

When I settled down, I became a social worker and stayed with it for twenty-six years. During those years I traveled extensively in the U.S. and in Europe observing how foreign governments work and comparing them to our U. S. government. I learned that I was quite conservative. Combining my conservative nature and my penchant for politics along with a rich imagination, I titled my short story *I Won*.

Holly Kaulitz Thieleman

> *Some are born great, some achieve greatness, and some have greatness thrust upon them.*
>
> —William Shakespeare.

This quote is one of Holly's favorites. It is her inspiration not only in writing but also in everyday life. She was born in Jacksonville, Arkansas, into a United States Air Force family. At an early age, Holly was bitten by the *travel bug*. She spent the first four years of her life in England, before moving back to the states in 1992 where she lived in Washington State before settling in Illinois in 2001.

Holly was always creative from childhood straight into adulthood. In her youth, she fell in love with writing. She is creative and full of ideas. Over the past few years, Holly has gained confidence in her writing style.

Many successful authors say they have one thing that helps influence their writing. Thieleman's main influence is music, which plays a huge part in her writing today. She finds influence from everything around her; televisions, movies, even the changing seasons help her to identify ideas for future works.

Working on a piece derived from her cultural heritage, Holly has become a stronger, enthusiastic writer. She continues to learn and develop as an author. Holly is a member of the Ocular Voices writers group. To connect with Holly you can e-mail her at musicmadness1@live.com.

About the Editor

John W. Smith

John W. Smith was born in East St. Louis Illinois and reared in the Metro East. His love for comics introduced him to reading. In the third grade, he discovered "real books." Thanks to comics, he fell in love with science fiction and horror. He devoured book after book about creatures of the night and other monsters. His reading sparked an interest in writing.

He received his degree in journalism and honed his abilities in public affairs with the U.S. Air Force. Retiring in 1992, he bought a Harley and began promoting motorcycling freedom and safety through a variety of California magazines, as well as national and international publications.

About the Editor

In civilian life, he worked for the *Bakersfield Californian* newspaper in advertising. This taught him the importance of editing to reduce word count, yet carry a punch in your sentences.

He has started several "Great American Novels," but he enjoys writing short stories. He is attempting to create novel-length works, but it takes time as he writes each chapter as though it were a continuing short story.

John has contributed stories to *Words, An Anthology of Short Stories* (2011). He published his first book of short stories entitled *Nightmares of a Madman* (2013). John edited and coordinated *A Dark and Stormy Night, an anthology* (2014). His short story "Spirit Dagger" is available in electronic format at SmashWords.com and other sites. "Colonial Scum," a short story about revenge, will be released as an e-short story in the summer of 2014. "Hungry Things," his third e-short story will be available this fall.

In addition, John is currently working on a second short story book titled *Dark Dreams* and has two unnamed novels in progress.

Stay connected with John

www.johnwsmithauthor.com
writerphotographer1946@gmail.com

Other Books by Well Read Press

Nightmares of a Madman (2013)
From John W. Smith
A collection of dark, short stories. Available on Kindle and other electronic distributors.

"Spirit Dagger" *(2014)* by John W. Smith
A short story e-book available on Kindle, and other electronic distributors

A Dark and Stormy Night: An Anthology 2014
A compilation of short fiction based on the phrase "a dark and stormy night." Available on Kindle and other electronic distributors.

COMING SOON FROM WELL READ PRESS

"Colonial Scum"

An e-short story by John W. Smith with George Burbank

Dark Dreams

A collection of short stories

By John W. Smith

Made in the USA
Charleston, SC
03 August 2014